"You'd B̶ _____
Fall Dow̶̶̶ _____
Obviously Overheated," He Said.

If anyone had told Robin that she would end up being stranded on an island with a man whose smile would cause a grown woman to whimper, she never would have believed it.

Well, here *was* a man who could have stepped out of one of her fevered imaginings, and she didn't have a clue what to do or say. Everything that came out of her mouth sounded like something from an inexperienced schoolgirl.

"We should at least introduce ourselves," he said, "since it looks as if we're going to be living together for a few days."

"What do you mean, we'll be *living* together?" she managed to croak.

He grinned, which she found totally distracting. "Since this is the only house on the island, you don't have much choice."

Dear Reader,

Our 20th anniversary pledge to you, our devoted readers, is a promise to continue delivering passionate, powerful, provocative love stories from your favorite Silhouette Desire authors for all the years to come!

As an anniversary treat, we've got a special book for you from the incomparable Annette Broadrick. *Marriage Prey* is a romance between the offspring of two couples from Annette's earliest Desire books, which Silhouette reissued along with a third early Desire novel last month as *Maximum Marriage: Men on a Mission.* Bestselling author Mary Lynn Baxter brings you November's MAN OF THE MONTH...*Her Perfect Man.* A minister and a reformed party girl fall for each other in this classic opposites-attract love story. *A Cowboy's Gift* is the latest offering by RITA Award winner Anne McAllister in her popular CODE OF THE WEST miniseries.

Another RITA winner, Caroline Cross, delivers the next installment of the exciting Desire miniseries FORTUNE'S CHILDREN: THE GROOMS with *Husband—or Enemy?* Dixie Browning's miniseries THE PASSIONATE POWERS continues with *The Virgin and the Vengeful Groom,* part of our extra-sensual BODY & SOUL promotion. And Sheri WhiteFeather has created another appealing Native American hero in *Night Wind's Woman.*

So please join us in celebrating twenty glorious years of category romance by indulging yourself with all six of these compelling love stories from Silhouette Desire!

Enjoy!

Joan Marlow Golan

Joan Marlow Golan
Senior Editor, Silhouette Desire

Please address questions and book requests to:
Silhouette Reader Service
U.S.: 3010 Walden Ave., P.O. Box 1325, Buffalo, NY 14269
Canadian: P.O. Box 609, Fort Erie, Ont. L2A 5X3

Marriage Prey

ANNETTE BROADRICK

Silhouette Desire®

Published by Silhouette Books

America's Publisher of Contemporary Romance

To my beautiful granddaughter Carmen

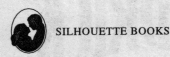 SILHOUETTE BOOKS

ISBN 0-373-76327-1

MARRIAGE PREY

Copyright © 2000 by Annette Broadrick

Visit Silhouette at www.eHarlequin.com

Printed in U.S.A.

Books by Annette Broadrick

ANNETTE BROADRICK

believes in romance and the magic of life. Since 1984, Annette has shared her view of life and love with readers. In addition to being nominated by *Romantic Times Magazine* as one of the Best New Authors of that year, she has also won the *Romantic Times* Reviewers' Choice Award for Best in its Series; the *Romantic Times* W.I.S.H. award; and the *Romantic Times Magazine* Lifetime Achievement Awards for Series Romance and Series Romantic Fantasy.

Dear Reader,

When I wrote my first three Desire novels fifteen years ago, not even my crystal ball (uncertain at best) could have hinted that they would be made a part of Silhouette's twentieth anniversary celebration in the year 2000. Nor could I possibly have guessed that I would have written over fifty novels by that date.

We wanted this celebration to be something special in the Desire line, and I decided it would be fun to check in with two of my earlier stories, and find out what the next generation was up to. So here is a chance to catch up on the characters from *Hunter's Prey* and *Bachelor Father.*

I'm always surprised to discover how real my characters are in my mind, as though they have, in fact, continued on with their lives while I've been busy telling other stories. It was fun to meet the adult Steve Antonelli from California and to learn about his life. It wasn't difficult to see where Robin McAlister of Texas might suddenly appear in Steve's life and turn it upside down. We certainly wouldn't want this particular hunk to become too complacent or to imagine that he might be in control of his own destiny!

I hope you enjoy reading their story as much as I enjoyed telling it.

Sincerely,

Annette Broadrick

One

Steve Antonelli stirred in his sleep, vaguely aware that there was something wrong.

He pulled one of his pillows over his head and burrowed back to his very erotic dream. For the past couple of months, ever since he'd returned to Los Angeles from his exotic island vacation, Steve had dreamed the same dream every night—the dream that whisked him back to his tropical paradise and all the memories he'd made there.

But the dream was gone.

Something wasn't right.

His normally dark bedroom—with its thick shades and lined drapes always closed—glowed with an unnatural brightness.

It couldn't be morning. Not yet.

And even if it were morning, he did not have to get up. He had the day off. A few weeks back at work as a homicide detective with the LAPD was enough to erase all thought of his vacation, at least during the day.

Now even his dreams were being disturbed.

Although still more than half asleep, Steve knew he wasn't in danger. The highly technological alarm system he'd had installed in his late-model condominium would have alerted him to a possible intruder.

So what was going on with the light he couldn't seem to escape?

He groaned, tossed the pillow aside and rolled over onto his back, the sheet wrapping around his bare hips.

Steve shoved his hair out of his face and opened his eyes against the unaccustomed glare.

What he saw caused him to jackknife into a sitting position.

Three men stood around the bed—one on each side and the third at the end. From Steve's vantage point, all three looked to be well over six feet tall. They could have been made from the same cookie cutter.

Each one was broad-shouldered and lean-hipped, with long legs covered in tight-fitting denim jeans.

Each one wore a large, silver belt buckle that should be listed as a lethal weapon.

Each one stood with legs apart and arms folded over heavily muscled chests.

Each one had a look in his eye and an expression on his face that caused Steve a moment of unease.

Well, maybe more than a moment. If he didn't know better, he would say they looked like three avenging men with a mission.

"What the—" he began, reaching for the pistol that was never far from his reach.

It wasn't there. The man standing to his right reached behind himself and lifted the pistol from the top of the dresser as though answering Steve's question, before he carefully placed it back on the dresser.

Now Steve really did feel naked. Not having any clothes on was one thing, but not having his protection was another thing entirely.

"Who the hell are you?" he demanded.

The man who stood at the bottom of the bed—who appeared slightly older and that much meaner than the others—continued to stare at him for a long moment of silence, then asked, "You Steve Antonelli?" in a low drawl that sounded as unhurried as the man appeared.

His alarm increasing with every breath he took, Steve demanded, "How did you get in here?"

The designated speaker glanced to the man on Steve's left. "Jim circumvented your system. Quite a sophisticated unit you've got hooked up here, according to him. We're impressed."

Steve dropped his face into his hands, his elbows propped on his knees. Was this some kind of dream he was having? Was this his punishment for the highly charged sexual dream he'd been thoroughly enjoying? He scrubbed his face with his hands and cautiously looked up.

All three men were still there, standing in the glow of the overhead light like hunters eyeing their prey.

Steve got the distinct impression that *he* was the prey.

Nobody had made any threatening moves toward him, but he certainly hadn't gotten the impression that they were there to sell him Avon cosmetics, either. He felt strangely unalarmed, though, in spite of the weird circumstances.

"Are you going to tell me who you are and why you're here?" he finally asked through gritted teeth.

"When you tell us if you're Steve Antonelli," his uninvited visitor replied.

"Of course I'm Steve," he yelled. "You could have gotten that off my mailbox. Now tell me who you are and what you want!"

The three men looked at each other, then back at Steve. Their obvious spokesman said, "We're here to personally deliver your invitation to attend our sister's wedding next week in Texas."

Now he knew he was dreaming. A bunch of strangers show up in his bedroom, wake him up—he checked his watch; it was barely seven o'clock—and now had the audacity to mention somebody's wedding they wanted him to attend? No way this could really be happening.

He fell back on the bed, rolled over—burying his head in his pillow once more—and muttered, "Shut the light out when you leave, okay?"

He knew when he woke up he'd enjoy telling his buddy, Ray, about the most ridiculous dream he'd had in a long, long time. He was supposed to meet Ray later this morning for brunch at their favorite restaurant on Sunset Boulevard, but he still had a couple of hours before he had to get up.

"Nice try, pal," the older one said from somewhere near his feet. "We're here to make sure you don't miss the wedding. How about getting dressed and packed so we can get out of here?"

Steve opened one eye enough so he could see the legs of the man standing beside him. This particular dream was slowly turning into a nightmare. The men were still there.

He sat up and threw off the sheet, stood without bothering to shield his bare body from them and said in his most polite voice, ''If you'll excuse me, gentlemen,'' and stalked into the bathroom, slamming the door behind him.

Steve leaned on the counter and stared into the mirror, his bloodshot eyes blearily staring back.

What could have caused him to have such a bizarre dream? He rubbed his prickly jaw, then slowly straightened, staring at his lean form. His body still bore the signs of his recent stay on a tropical beach—deeply tanned except for the area around his hips. He rubbed his taut stomach, then scratched his chest, reflexively. Was he finally losing it after all these years on the force?

A three-week vacation should have been long enough for him to clear his head, catch up on his rest and learn to eat three meals a day with some degree of regularity. He'd returned home ready to face his real life again.

Part of that routine was meeting Ray in a few hours for their weekly get-together. With a slight shake of his head, Steve turned on the shower and waited while the water warmed before stepping under the strong spray and forcing his body and brain to wake up beneath the steady onslaught.

By the time he dried off, shaved, brushed his teeth and hair Steve finally felt he was ready to laugh off his early-morning delusion and get on with his day.

He threw open the door into the bedroom and strode toward his closet. Halfway there he came to an abrupt halt.

Three men stood shoulder to shoulder in a line between him and the door to the rest of the condo.

Whatever was going on, this was no dream. He would just have to deal with whatever crazy stunt he'd been made a part of.

"I give up," he said, throwing up his hands. "You've got me. Now tell me who hired you guys for this practical joke. Was it Ray? I'll admit I never thought he had this much imagination, but I'll admit he's good. You three look like you just came off the Universal lot of a Western town. All you need are six guns strapped to your hips."

The spokesman of the trio glanced at the other two. "Can you believe this guy, pretending he doesn't know Robin?"

Steve stared at them, unable to get his tongue wrapped around a coherent word. Finally, he managed a rather strangled rendition of the word "Robin?" He cleared his throat. "Are you by any chance talking about Robin McAlister?"

The men looked at him approvingly. "I'm glad to see your memory's improving," the one called Jim muttered.

"There's nothing wrong with my memory. What I don't understand is what Robin has to do with you characters."

"Well," said the third man who had been silent up until now, "it's this way. We're Robin's brothers and we're just here to make real sure that you show up at our sister's wedding next week...since you're going to be the groom."

Two

Steve let himself into his condo, turned off the alarm and then wearily entered the kitchen. He couldn't remember the last time he'd eaten. He was so tired that nothing sounded good.

He opened the refrigerator and snagged a bottle of beer, his own form of a sleeping potion—one beer on an empty stomach would have him out in no time.

The blinking light on his telephone registered three calls. He punched the replay button and listened.

"Hi, Steve," a sexy female voice said. He frowned, then recognized Alicia's voice as she continued. "I haven't heard from you in weeks, honey. I know how busy you've been, but I miss you. Give me a call, okay?

Anytime. Day or night." She ended with a breathy chuckle.

"Yo, Steve, buddy, give me a call, okay?" followed by a dial tone was the next message. Ray. He'd had to cancel their last two scheduled get-togethers.

The third call made him straighten. It was his father. "Steve, give me a call whenever you get in tonight, will you please?"

Steve glanced at his watch. It was past eleven o'clock, but then, his dad was never one to go to bed early. He reached for the phone and hit the speed dial number. His dad answered on the first ring.

"What's wrong?" Steve asked as soon as his dad answered.

"That's what I want to know," Tony Antonelli replied.

Steve frowned. "I don't know what you're talking about, Dad. Your call sounded urgent."

"It was. I'm concerned about you, Steve. You've canceled out on the last two family dinners your mother planned. Today was really important to her. I need to know what's going on with you."

Steve dropped his chin on his chest and slumped against the kitchen cabinets. "It's just work, Dad."

"You're letting it get to you, son," his dad replied softly.

Steve rubbed his forehead and felt the ridges between his eyes. "This one was only five years old, Dad. *Five.* She was out playing in her yard and got strafed by a gang shooting. I'm going to get them for that, I don't care how long it takes."

"I understand. I really do. And I admire your dedication, but, son, you've got to take some time off or you're going to end up as another statistic somewhere—

of burnout, if nothing else. I know you aren't eating right or getting enough sleep. You've got to do something to get out of this rut you've built for yourself."

Steve kneaded the muscles in his neck. "Yeah. I know."

"Today was supposed to be your day off, wasn't it?"

"Yeah."

"So when was the last time you actually took your days off?"

"I can't remember."

"Uh-huh. How about Christmas? It's coming up in a couple of weeks. Can we count on your being here?"

Steve smiled. "I'll be there. I promise."

Tony's voice sounded gruff. "Good. I love you, son."

"I love you, too, Dad," he replied. They hung up.

Steve climbed the stairs and left a trail of clothes across his bedroom floor and into the bathroom. He stayed under the hot stinging water of a shower until the water began to cool, then dried off and fell into bed.

His last thought was a reminder that he really needed to get a life.

Austin, Texas

"Just think about it, Robin, ten days away from everything we've ever known," Cindi Brenham said with an ecstatic sigh. "Ten whole days cruising the Caribbean with nothing to do but eat all that fabulous food, flirt with the extremely eligible men who will no doubt look like male models. We'll break their hearts, work on our tans and then come back here to finish our last semester before graduation. Let's face it, we owe it to ourselves to have a little fun during our break."

Cindi sat across from Robin McAlister at a small out-

door café near the University of Texas campus. Despite
the calendar proclaiming it to be the middle of December,
the weather was sunny and warm.

Robin studied her vivacious friend. Sometimes she
wondered how two people so opposite in temperament
and looks could be so close, but she and Cindi had been
friends since their first day of school in Cielo, a small
town in the western hills of Texas. They had never ques-
tioned their friendship as they'd gone from grade school
to middle school to high school together. No one had
found it in the least surprising that they'd chosen to go
to the same university as roommates.

Cindi planned to make her mark in the booming com-
puter industry, while Robin had set her sights in the field
of public relations. They'd already spent the past two
summers interning in those fields and were looking forward to getting out in the world in a few short months.

In the meantime they were impatient to break out of
their current educational routine and do something totally
different.

Robin sighed. "It sounds too good to be true, Cindi.
Are you sure you understood your mother correctly?"

Cindi bobbed her head, her black curls dancing around
her face. "Aunt Nell bought and paid for two tickets on
a cruise leaving January 5 and returning January 15, but
Uncle Frank is in the hospital recovering from a heart
attack. There's no way they can go, and it's too late to
get their money back. It's a perfect opportunity for us."

It sounded wonderful to Robin. A chance to get away
for a while…a chance to be on her own. The idea of
getting away from her three overprotective brothers
sounded increasingly enticing, the more she thought
about it.

She loved her family, of course. Nobody could have

more loving and generous parents than her mom and dad. Robin felt blessed to have inherited her mother's tall, slender figure, her red hair and her green eyes. Her mother had been a famous model before she had her family, and Robin had actually had a couple of offers to model herself since she'd been away at school. Of course, by then she'd known not to mention the offers to her family, especially her father.

Robin hadn't expected, once she became a teenager, that her loving and normally easygoing dad would suddenly become a frowning, possessive guardian. What was worse, as she continued to grow and mature, he trained her brothers to watch over her like three ferocious guardian angels.

Jason was the oldest at twenty-eight. He'd been named after their dad. Jim just turned twenty-five and Robin was almost twenty-two. Josh was the baby of the family at nineteen.

Robin had hoped her brothers would relax their vigil once she went off to college, but it hadn't worked out that way. Jim was still in college at UT back then. By the time he graduated Josh had come along to take over the task of protective male in her life. It was enough to make her consider going over the wall and doing something completely crazy at times. Such as impulsively going on a Caribbean cruise in the middle of winter.

"So, what do you think?" Cindi said, impatiently. "Don't you think it would be a perfect break from all this studying?"

Robin nodded slowly, her thoughts churning. "Not only that," she said, "there's no way any of my brothers could get a ticket this late. I would actually be getting a chance to do something on my own without someone

constantly hovering around me, scaring off any prospects
for dates, like they've done for the past several years.''

Cindi grinned. "Oh, I don't know. If I thought I could
convince Jase to come with us—'' she began in a teasing
voice.

Robin rolled her eyes. Cindi's crush on Jason was the
worst-kept secret in the whole state. The fact that Jason
totally ignored Cindi never seemed to dampen her ardor.
Sometimes Robin wondered what Cindi would do if Jason suddenly showed her any attention. For all her bold
talk, she'd probably run for the border.

"Then you'll do it?" Cindi asked. "I told Mom I'd
call her back tonight and let her know if we could go.''

"What should I tell my folks? I'm fairly certain my
dad's not going to like the idea," Robin said, thinking
out loud.

"Then wait until just before we go. I mean, he never
likes not knowing exactly where you are and whom
you're with, so what else is new? But what could be safer
than a cruise? We'll be rooming together. So we'll be
keeping each other company and out of mischief. Besides, you're an adult now. He's got to let go sometime.''

"Uh-huh," Robin replied with more than a hint of
skepticism. "You know that. I know that. But as far as
my dad is concerned, I'm still the toddler he used to carry
around on his shoulders or in front of him on his horse.
It's a wonder my brothers didn't hate me, the way he was
always carrying on about his one and only daughter.''

Cindi grinned. "I think it's sweet, myself. Let's face
it, behind that gruff exterior, your dad is a pushover. He's
never been able to say no to you for long. His first
glimpse of tears and he surrenders.''

"So if I wait to tell him until just before we leave,
you think he'll take it better?''

"Nope. You just won't have to listen to him for as long. By the time you get back, he'll have calmed down a little. Maybe."

Robin laughed. "Yep, that's my dad, all right."

"We also have time to shop for cruise clothes. Oh, Robin! This is going to be the greatest time of our lives! We'll look back on this later and tell our grandkids about the time we took off to explore the islands in a cruise ship."

"Let's just hope neither one of us gets seasick."

Cindi stood, dropping a tip on the table for the waitress. "Well, we're about to find out, aren't we?"

Santa Monica, California
December 28

"Let's face it, Steve," Ray said, walking off the court after they finished their last game of tennis. "You've been working too hard and you're out of shape. I can't believe you missed that last one." He slapped Steve on the back. "I never thought I'd see the day when I could beat you so consistently. Let's face it, ol' buddy, you aren't the challenge you used to be."

"Stuff it, Cassidy. I'm just off my game today. Wait until next time. I'll show you all the challenge you can handle."

"Maybe, but if you ask me, what you need is some time off—a vacation."

Steve grabbed the towel lying with his bag and wiped it over his face. Then he picked up his bottle of water and drank half of it before pausing. He looked around the area, admiring the intense blue of the sky and the way the palm trees stood out in stark relief.

"You're ignoring me," Ray said after a few minutes.

"Actually, I'm thinking about what you just said. I happen to agree with you."

"Which part? That you're out of shape or that you need a vacation?"

"Both, actually. It just so happens that an old friend of my dad was visiting with the folks in Santa Barbara while I was home last week. He was talking to me about taking some time off and visiting his island in the Virgin Islands."

"His *island?* Are you serious? He owns the entire thing?"

Steve shrugged. "He used to play ball with dad, invested his money over the years and decided to retire to some exotic, out-of-the-way place. He said he and his wife lasted there about nine months before they both agreed that Eden wasn't all it was cracked up to be. No malls, no ESPN, no friends and family. So they use it for a getaway weekend once in a while, but most of the time the only ones living there is the native family who looks after the property. He told me the place was just waiting there, begging to be used."

Ray sat down on the bench and looked up at Steve in awe. "How come my family doesn't know people who own islands?" he asked with a grin. "Do you think you'll take him up on the offer?"

Steve sighed. "Actually, I talked to the captain yesterday about taking some time off. He's to get back with me after the holidays. I'm asking for three weeks, which will put a strain on covering my duties for so long."

"Wish I could go with you, but I don't have any time coming until May."

Steve picked up his bag. "Actually, I'm looking forward to being alone for a while. The more I think about it, the more the idea of going off by myself appeals to me. Not to have to make conversation with anyone, to be able to sleep whenever I want, to catch up on some reading, soak up some sun—it all sounds perfect to me."

"Won't you miss having some feminine companionship, playing Robinson Crusoe like that?"

Steve laughed and shook his head. "That's the last thing that sounds appealing to me right now. I think I finally managed to convince Alicia last night that there's no future for us, despite her best efforts to convince me otherwise. Solitude sounds downright enticing after being smothered by her these past few months."

"Too bad I don't have your good looks to go with my sparkling personality," Ray said solemnly. "Let's face it, pal. Those smoldering dark looks are wasted on you."

Steve studied his redheaded, freckle-faced friend and grinned. Ray was a chick magnet and he knew it, so all his talk was just so much baloney. "Give me a break," Steve replied. "You've got more women after you than any five men."

"Maybe," Ray admitted with a shrug. "But it's those Italian good looks of yours that get the second glances every time, my friend. That aloof air—not to mention the dimples and curly hair—seems to lure them into your vicinity even when you aren't aware of them. Such as now," he added ruefully.

Steve frowned. "What are you talking about?"

"Those two watching us leave the court," Ray replied, nodding to the young women taking over the court behind them. "They kept watching you during that last set as though trying to decide what TV show they'd seen you on."

Steve shook his head in disgust. "Very funny."

"You know, Steve, one of these days you're going to

lose that very guarded heart of yours, and when you do, you'll discover how the rest of us mortals feel.'' He grinned. ''I hope I'm around to watch when that happens.''

''I've told you, Ray. Being a cop doesn't lend itself to successful relationships. Every guy I work with who's been married is either divorced or catching hell at home because of his long hours and dangerous duties, not to mention the lousy pay.''

''So change jobs.''

''I like what I do. Most of the time. But ever since Christmas, I've been seriously considering taking a break. What is it about the holidays that bring the weirdest people out into the open to create mayhem on those around them? I don't guess I'll ever get used to man's inhumanity toward his fellow man.''

''I certainly hope not. Otherwise you'd lose your edge...and you're a damned good cop.''

''Tell my boss that. Maybe he'll finally put in for that raise that's overdue.''

They reached their cars, and Steve paused before getting into his. ''I'll let you know if I get the okay on this trip. And when I get back, we'll set up a rematch and see if I'm enough competition for you.''

''Promise you won't take a tennis racket with you.''

Steve laughed. ''And who would I be playing tennis with on a deserted island? I won't even be able to send you a postcard, I'll be so isolated.''

''I hope you get the time off,'' Ray said, suddenly serious. ''That's the first time I've heard you laugh in a long while. I'll enjoy seeing you with your sense of humor back.''

Miami, Florida
January 5

"Oh, Robin, this is awful," Cindi whispered dramatically as the two of them stood at the rail of the ship and watched the other guests of the cruise line come on board.

"Well, it isn't exactly what we were expecting, is it?" Robin responded ruefully.

"I haven't seen anyone younger than sixty, have you?"

"Do you suppose your aunt and uncle booked through some club or something?"

"I never thought of that. They'd fit right in with this group. So what are we going to do?"

Robin laughed. "We're going to enjoy ourselves, that's what. We're going to wear all our sexy new clothes, eat until we can hardly move and entertain ourselves with all those fantasies of good-looking men."

Cindi glanced over her shoulder. "Well, actually, I saw some crew members that weren't half-bad. Who knows? Maybe they'll take pity on us. Have you noticed that there aren't any single women? Every one of them is with a man."

"Maybe they know something we don't know. Maybe they got a special brochure that told them to bring their own male."

"Instead of a 'bring your own bottle' party, huh?"

"Something like that."

They looked at each other and started laughing. They were still laughing when one of the crew paused beside them and said, "We're glad to see you're enjoying yourselves so quickly. If you'd like some refreshments, I'll show you the way to the bar and lounge area."

Robin gave Cindi a quick glance, then said, "Sounds

great.'' As they followed the attendant, Robin acknowledged to herself the irony of their situation. Neither her father nor her brothers could possibly have reason to worry about her on this trip.

San Saba Island

Steve stood on the beach and watched the sky lighten, feeling the tension draining from his body. He'd been here three days, and the island was beginning to work its magic on him. The only sound was the soothing rhythm of the waves washing along the shoreline. An occasional bird called to its mate. Otherwise there was silence.

The silence had been the hardest difference to adjust to. There was no noise of traffic—sirens screaming, horns honking, brakes squealing. He couldn't remember a time in his recent past where those noises hadn't played a role in the background of his life.

Steve turned and looked up to the crest of the rise of land behind him, where the house looked out over the vista of sea and sky. No expense had been spared in turning the house into a tropical paradise. In addition to all the latest appliances to make the kitchen and laundry run smoothly, there were tiled floors with woven mats scattered throughout the house, floor-to-ceiling windows in every room, and a sense that movement was optional.

The ceiling paddle fans in each room stirred the air, their soft hum a quiet accompaniment to his thoughts as he'd struggled to find a routine that didn't call for him to be constantly on the move.

The first day he'd arrived—after flying through the night from Los Angeles to Miami, then changing planes in order to arrive eventually in St. Thomas, and then be taken by launch to San Saba Island—Steve had slept around the clock. He'd awakened late in the evening only to discover that he'd missed seeing much of the island in daylight.

He'd wandered through the house, looking into each room at the wicker and rattan furniture, the tropical print material covering the cushions, the quiet sense of time-lessness, of peace and serenity, and knew that he was a long way from L.A.

He'd found a tempting array of food in the refrigera-tor—fresh fruits and vegetables, as well as a plate that could be warmed in the microwave. Carmela had pre-pared the food while her husband, Romano, had met him in St. Thomas and brought him by boat to the island. They were happy people, obviously enjoying their way of life, pleased to be working for an American who rarely visited, delighted to be able to look after Steve.

On the boat ride over to San Saba, Romano had given him a brief history of the island. He'd explained that, even at the highest point on the island, there was no sign of the other islands that made up the chain strung along the sea like green jewels on a blue background that he'd seen from the air when he'd flown in. He would be alone for the first time in his life, to do what he wished to do, or to do nothing, if it pleased him.

Since he'd first arrived on the island, Steve had seen little of the caretakers, although his meals were always prepared and waiting for him and his clothes were placed, freshly laundered, in his room each day.

A guy could definitely get used to this existence.

His stomach growled and he laughed softly to himself. Carmela was a fantastic cook, and his body had quickly adapted to the regular meals that she so appetizingly pre-pared for him. Romano had explained that he traveled to St. Thomas periodically for supplies. As a result Steve ate like an Eastern potentate. At the rate he was going he wouldn't be surprised if he gained ten pounds by the time he returned home.

Once the sun broke above the horizon, flooding the water and the sky with brilliant rays, Steve was ready to return to the house. After breakfast he intended to do some exploring of the island, then take another long nap. He'd already gotten more sleep in these past few days than he'd had in weeks.

He began the trek up the path to the house.

Robin and Cindi had been on the ten-day cruise for three days when the activities director announced that the guests on board were invited to take one of the boats over to a nearby island that was well-known for its tide pools and exotic species from the sea.

Cindi wasn't interested in tide pools, but Robin at the last minute thought it might be fun to join the small group planning to participate. She pulled out one of her small tote bags, and threw into it an extra swimsuit besides the one she wore under her shirt and shorts, a large beach towel, added a pair of slacks and a windbreaker in case it got cooler before they returned and joined the group who wanted to visit the island. She had not signed up, so she was not on the list of cruise members going to the island, but she was assured one more would not matter.

On their way the officer in charge explained that an American owned the island. He had agreed to allow the cruise ship company access to the island as long as they stayed on the northern shore. The private residence was at the other end of the island, which was off-limits to cruise passengers.

Robin didn't care. It felt good to leave the ship for a few hours. She'd discovered that she felt cooped up on board, even though the luxury liner was huge. It was probably a psychological effect, knowing that she had to stay on the ship. Their first day trip was scheduled for St. Croix, which was still a few days away. She was ready to get on solid ground, if only for a few hours.

Once they landed, Robin wandered with the others as they followed the ship's officer's lecture regarding the various sea creatures that had made their homes in the shallow tidal pools among the rocks. When he was finished, the group scattered to explore the area.

Robin lost track of time as she became absorbed in the pools. She climbed over rocks and followed the rim where sand and sea met, watching the activity of the tiny specimens with awe.

When she heard the boat's bell signaling time for their return, she was startled to discover that she had wandered much farther down the beach than the others. She grabbed her bag and ran, clambering over outcroppings of rocks that blocked her view of the rest of the island and her fellow passengers.

In her hurry she slipped and fell, scraping her foot against some sharp shells imbedded in the rock, which further delayed her. When she finally made it around the curve of vegetation that grew down to the sea at the place where they'd come ashore, Robin was horrified to see the launch had already left and was rapidly disappearing over the horizon.

"No-o-o-o-o!" she cried, jumping up and down. "Come back! Help!" She limped along the shore, waving and calling, but no one noticed her.

She'd been warned, of course. The ship kept a tight schedule. The passengers were often reminded that the tide waited on no one, and if a passenger failed to meet the time schedule, they would be left. And they didn't have her on the roster, so they wouldn't have waited a few seconds longer, anyway.

It had never occurred to her that she would be one of those people left behind.

What in the world was she going to do? She looked around at the idyllic setting—the softly curving beach of fine, white sand; the thick tropical vegetation vibrantly green against the blue backdrop of cloudless sky; the cool water with its lacy foam washing against the sand.   Unfortunately, at that particular moment she couldn't really appreciate the beauty of the place.

Fighting her panic, Robin watched as the launch disappeared from view.

She sat down on the sand and burst into tears of frustration and anger at herself. How could she have been so oblivious of the time and distance she'd gone? She'd been an absolute fool, and now would have to pay the consequences.

At least she knew that someone had a home on the island if she could find the courage to go looking for him. It wasn't as if she were on a deserted island and forced to forage for food in order to survive. Even if cruise passengers weren't allowed to bother the owner, she felt certain he would understand her dilemma and help her in some way.

The question was, how was she going to get back to the ship?

If people lived here, there must be some form of communication. If she could find a phone or a ham radio, she'd be able to contact the cruise ship and find out what she had to do in order to rejoin the cruise.

Her busy thoughts kept pace with her footsteps. There was no reason to panic, after all. She could deal with this just fine.

However, she was thankful that none of her brothers knew what had happened to her. If they ever found out about this—and she planned to do everything in her power to make certain they never did—they would be convinced they'd been right all along.

She couldn't be trusted to stay out of trouble on her own.

Three

Steve had been on the island for seven full days now and had to admit to himself that he wasn't certain he would ever be eager to return to civilization. He hadn't fully realized how driven he'd been on the job until he'd adapted his new schedule to the sun since coming to the island.

He got up at daybreak, spent his day outside—either swimming, reading or napping—and went to bed not long after the sun set. This was what man was intended to do, he thought to himself—follow nature's rhythms. He ate whenever he was hungry, slept whenever the mood struck him and hadn't looked at a timepiece since he'd set foot on the island.

His routine was simple. By dawn he would be on the shore, watching the sunrise. Later he would swim in the lagoon, working up an appetite for breakfast. After breakfast he explored the island, a new section each day. He'd found hidden waterfalls and small ponds surrounded by ferns, animal trails that led from one side of the island to the other, fruits growing wild.

For the first time since he could remember, he woke up each morning eager to face the day.

Now as he reached one of the high points on the north side of the island, his binoculars in hand, Steve knew he owed a real debt of gratitude to Ed for suggesting he use his place. Steve would be eternally grateful.

He paused, thinking he saw something on the horizon. He focused the glasses and smiled. His first sight of the existence of civilization since he's arrived—a cruise ship appeared in his sights, somewhere off in the distance.

Steve recalled that Ed had mentioned an arrangement he'd made with one of the cruise lines where the passengers were allowed to visit the island for a few hours every couple of weeks. Ed had assured Steve that he wouldn't be disturbed. He was curious to know if there had been recent visitors or whether he could expect some in the next few hours. He scanned the beach, but with his first visual sweep didn't spot anyone.

He raised his binoculars to the water again and checked to see if he could spot any dolphins frolicking about. The sea fascinated him. He could watch it for hours.

It was when he lowered the glasses some time later that he caught movement on the beach out of the corner of his eye.

He refocused and looked through the glasses once again. There, standing on the shore facing out to sea was the figure of a tall, slender female wearing a halter top and shorts, with a large straw hat perched on her head. A carryall rested at her canvas-shod feet. She was the very picture of dejection.

He looked through the strong glasses toward the cruise ship and spotted a smaller craft rapidly approaching it. Oops. From his perspective on the high point overlooking the island and the ocean, the situation appeared obvious. Somehow the woman had missed the launch and her ride back to the cruise ship.

She was stranded on the island.

Steve quickly realized that it was up to him to do something. He was surprised to discover that he wasn't as irritated as he might have imagined he would be to have his solitary vacation interrupted by an intruder. Like Adam in the Garden of Eden, he had grown somewhat lonely, a fact that hadn't announced itself until he saw the dejected woman on the beach.

No doubt this wasn't the first time someone had missed his or her ride during one of these outings. Romano would be able to tell them how to get her back to her ship.

Even as he watched, he could see the cruise ship moving over the horizon, its smokestacks growing smaller until they finally disappeared from view.

Yep, she was well and truly stranded, at least for now.

Steve wondered how long she'd been standing there looking out to sea. Did she really think that by staring after the disappearing ship—and it must have already dropped out of sight from where she stood—through sheer willpower she could mentally coerce someone to come to her rescue?

As though she heard his thoughts, the woman slowly turned and surveyed the island behind her, tilting her head upward so that for the first time he saw her face— her young, exquisitely shaped, delicately featured face.

His heart took off like a war drum stirring up the natives.

Not a good sign.

Being a red-blooded male, Steve wasn't going to deny that he noticed what a woman looked like, but he'd never before had this kind of reaction at his first sight of an attractive woman. After all, he hadn't been alone *that* long!

It was much too corny to say she looked like an angel, but the thought actually crossed his mind. The softly tinted tan that covered her body couldn't hide her fair complexion. Wisps of red curled around her cheeks and ears, the only hint he had of her hair color.

Even with the high-powered binoculars he couldn't see the color of her eyes, but they were light, and if he wasn't mistaken they were currently spilling tears down her cheeks as she sat down forlornly.

Definitely a damsel in distress, if he'd ever seen one.

Well, Steve, old boy, here's your chance to play hero.

Now that he'd gotten a better look at her, he wasn't at all certain he was ready to have the serene existence he'd adopted while on the island disrupted by an unusually attractive woman. He'd been living an easy life—shaving whenever his beard began to itch, living in the briefest of his swim attire, not having to take another person's whims into consideration.

It had been his experience that the more attractive a woman was, the more she expected her whims to be met, as though her beauty entitled her to special consideration. That attitude had always irritated him and he hoped to hell this woman wasn't some kind of prima donna who was going to take her irritation out on him because she'd missed her ride.

The very fact that she'd missed that ride suggested that she didn't think the rules were intended for her.

He sighed. Regardless, he couldn't leave her stranded

on the beach, so he might as well get down there and make his presence known.

Since there was no trail down to that part of the island from where he stood, he would have to retrace his steps to about midisland, then follow the beach to where she was. Not that it mattered. She wasn't going anywhere anytime soon, that was certain.

Robin felt like a fool. How could she have wandered so far from the rest of them without noticing? How could she have been so caught up in her explorations that she forgot to watch the time? And why did she have to be such a klutz and fall, further delaying her?

She limped over to the shade of the thick jungle vegetation and sat down. She needed to take stock of her situation and decide what to do.

After removing her hat, she wiped her brow and scrubbed the tears from her face with her towel.

She had no one else to blame but herself, so she might as well stop feeling sorry for herself and decide how she was going to approach the owner of the island and ask him for assistance.

She gave herself a pep talk. It could be worse, she supposed.

Positive thought number one: she didn't have to worry about frostbite.

Positive thought number two: despite Cindi's teasing that she wasn't going on a six-week safari when she'd been getting ready for this outing, Robin had brought several items with her that might prove to be useful, depending on how long she was stranded here.

Which was another thing. She needed to remember what the passengers had been told they were to do if they missed the deadlines for reboarding. All she could recall was the stern admonition to be on time, which didn't help much at the moment.

In the meantime, she would look at what she had brought with her, and how it would help in her new situation. She opened her bag and carefully removed each item, one by one.

Her sunshades and her suntan lotion.

Since she never went anywhere without her supply of lotion, its inclusion was a given. Thanks to her mother, she had fair skin that had to be slathered with the highest UV protection on the market today. Even so, she'd managed to acquire more of a tan than she'd ever had before.

So far only Cindi had been there to admire it. However, there had been the possibility that during one of their ports of call she might meet some tall, dark stranger who would sweep her off her feet—all the while admiring her luscious tan, mind you—and show her all sorts of sinfully delicious pleasures that she'd been denied up until now because of her overprotective family.

The only problem with that scenario was that now she wouldn't have the chance to meet anyone. If she remembered the itinerary correctly, the ship would not be coming back this way for a week, when it was headed toward home port. And what if the ship didn't stop for another visit to this island on the return trip?

What if she was stranded here forever?

Okay, so *forever* was a little strong, she thought. No need to panic, after all. She reminded herself that there was a house somewhere on the island. If there was a house, there were bound to be people, right?

Right.

And she was going to go knock on the door like Little Red Riding Hood—or was that Goldilocks?—and ask for help.

There really was no help for it.

She dug into her pack once again.

The shirt she had worn to the island was folded inside, plus the slacks, windbreaker and second swimsuit.

Oh, great. No underwear.

A brush, a comb and a few cosmetic necessities.

Okay, so Cindi had been right about unnecessary items, but, boy, was she glad she'd thrown her cosmetic bag in. She actually had her small, folding toothbrush and paste in a travel size that she'd never had occasion to use.

At the bottom of the bag she found food. An apple, a pear, two oranges, two granola bars and a bottle of water.

That should hold her for at least—oh, maybe three to four hours.

Who was she kidding? She was marooned on an island for an undetermined number of days. She certainly didn't have enough supplies to survive without seeking help.

She would have to explore the island and hope that the natives were friendly.

She glanced up at the sun. It was definitely sliding toward the west. With a sigh of resignation, Robin stood, dusted off her shorts, placed her straw hat squarely on her head, shouldered her bag and lifted her shoulders.

She could do this. She was strong. She was self-reliant. She was woman!

Already feeling better with that little pep talk, she faced south and the unknown. She caught sight of movement in the distance.

Speaking of natives, she was just about to meet one of them.

His long stride carried him rapidly toward her as he trod the hard-packed sand near the edge of the water. For just a second Robin had an almost ungovernable urge to

hide in the vegetation before her common sense pre-
vailed. For one thing his purposeful strides made it clear
he had already seen her and was coming to meet her. For
another, she really did need some help.

She whipped out her sunshades and put them on, feeling better able to cope with a stranger behind the shields.
Her mother had always told her that her eyes mirrored
her every thought. She had no desire to let this stranger
in on what she was thinking.

Especially about him.

As he drew closer, Robin's pulse accelerated. If he was
a sample of the natives around here, all she could say
was wow.

Double wow.

The only article of clothing he wore was a faded pair
of swim trunks that clung to his hips and thighs, lovingly
molding their muscled shape. He was darkly tanned—
almost bronzed—by the sun. His wide shoulders tapered
to a trim waist and—

There she was, staring at his only article of clothing
again.

Robin quickly glanced down his strongly muscled legs
and noticed he wore boat shoes.

"You seem to be lost," were his first words as he
came to a stop in front of her. She continued to stare at
him. She couldn't help it. She hadn't moved since she'd
first spotted him.

Many of her friends teased her about growing up with
a bunch of good-looking brothers, and it was true that a
handsome male didn't easily impress her.

So what was the matter with her?

Now that he was up close she could see that this was
a man, not a boy. He looked to be in his thirties. Experience had left tiny lines around his eyes and mouth. His

dark eyes were shuttered. His black, curly hair gave a boyish air to a man who seemed too serious to be in the habit of smiling much.

She smiled, hoping to ease the tension that had sprung up as soon as he spoke. "Not lost, exactly. Marooned would be a more accurate description."

He nodded toward the water. "You're a passenger on the cruise ship?"

"I was."

"And you missed the launch."

"I suppose this happens to you all the time," she said, her smile fading slightly when he didn't respond to it. He stood there with his hands resting lightly on his hips, his legs apart, looking at her as though she was an unidentified specimen he'd found washed up on the beach.

Robin was not used to a man looking at her with such detached objectivity. Not that she was vain about her looks, but she'd grown used to being given a second glance by newcomers. It was that reaction by most men that had caused her brothers to appoint themselves her guardians. When they were around her, Robin never had to worry about being pursued by an unsavory character. They made certain that no one dared to follow up on an introduction.

Now, here she was, free of her brothers' interference, able to respond to a very attractive male if he showed any interest in her, only to discover that she'd made no impression on him whatsoever.

What a revolting development that was, she decided when he continued to watch her as though waiting for her to say something.

"I, uh, I presume that you're the owner of the island," she finally said.

"Nope," he replied cheerfully enough. "Just visiting."

"Oh. Well. Do you by any chance have a phone I could use?"

He grinned, and Robin hated the idea that she found him so very attractive. He had a killer smile, more potent because this was the first time he'd used it. "Whom do you intend to call?" he asked with genuine curiosity.

Good question. "Well, maybe I could contact the ship. At least I need to let my roommate know I didn't drown. Then maybe figure out what I can do next."

He turned and started back up the beach. "Sure. Come on. I'll show you the way to the house. It's at the other end of the island. Hope you don't mind a hike."

He didn't bother to wait to see if she was going to follow him, which she thought was somewhat rude. However, she didn't suppose it would do her much good to conduct lessons on manners at this point.

She trotted to catch up with him. "Have you been here long?" she asked, hoping to show a polite interest in him.

"Nope."

She waited but he didn't say anything more.

They walked for some time in silence before she said, "You aren't much of a conversationalist, are you?"

Without breaking stride or looking at her, he said, "I came here to get away from people."

"Oh." After another few minutes, she added, "I truly am sorry for inconveniencing you."

"You aren't."

Maybe not, but he was making it clear that her appearance on the island wasn't something he particularly wanted.

At least they had that much in common.

He set a killing pace along the shore. By the time they

eventually began to climb the path that led up to the house, Robin was breathing hard but too stubborn to ask him to slow down.

When they reached the top, she paused and stared at the house in awe. It was one story but seemed to go off on several angles, following the curve of the cliff. The view from any of the many windows must be absolutely spectacular. Whoever had built the place hadn't been short of money.

When they reached the patio with its comfortably padded chaise lounges and tables, she almost threw herself down on one of the chairs in relief. Instead, she looked at him, waiting for his next move.

It wasn't long in coming. "Do you know the phone number of the ship?" he asked.

Why was it he kept making her feel like a complete fool?

"I, well, no, actually I don't."

He frowned and stepped closer, peering at her from under the brim of her hat. "You'd better sit down before you fall down. You're flushed and obviously over-heated."

She thought of several responses, all sarcastic, that she could make. Instead she sat down and watched as he disappeared into the house.

Robin leaned her head back and closed her eyes. If anyone had told her, when she and Cindi decided to go on this cruise, that she would end up being stranded on an island with a stern-looking man whose unexpected smile would cause a grown woman to whimper, she would never have believed it.

Hadn't they fantasized about all the men they would meet on this cruise? They'd chatted about what they hoped their dream male would look like, how she and

Cindi would flirt and eventually break each man's heart because—after all—all they wanted was a vacation flirtation. Nothing permanent. Nothing serious.

Well, here was a man who could have stepped out of one of her fevered imaginings, and she didn't have a clue what to do or say. Everything that came out of her mouth sounded like something from an awkward, inexperienced schoolgirl.

This was so embarrassing. She'd managed to crash this man's quiet vacation and now had to make the best of it.

Well. She would get back to the ship as quickly as possible. There must be a way. This man must have some kind of transportation. If he would offer it. So far he was being polite. Minimally polite. She supposed that was the most she could expect.

She heard the whisper of the sliding glass door as it opened and she glanced up. Her rescuer came toward her, followed by a woman of magnificent proportions carrying a tray filled with a pitcher of something frosty and wet.

"Here you go, missy," the woman said, placing the tray on a nearby table and handing Robin a tall glass filled with ice cubes and a pink liquid. Robin sipped and sighed with sublime satisfaction. The tart fruit drink was just what she needed.

"Thank you so much," Robin said with heartfelt gratitude. The woman smiled and left.

"We should at least introduce ourselves," the man said, sitting on the lounge next to her chair, "since it looks as if we're going to be living together for a few days."

It was unfortunate that Robin had just taken another large swallow of liquid when he spoke. Part of it went down her windpipe, causing her to choke. She sprayed her drink down the front of her halter top and began to cough.

He immediately jumped up and began to pound on her back with enthusiastic vigor.

"Please," she managed to gasp. "I'm fine." Even she knew she was far from fine. Her voice came out strangled, but he certainly wasn't helping anything.

When he sat down and looked at her again, he picked up a towel nearby and silently offered it to her. She'd managed to set her glass down without spilling it and now took the towel, wiping the tears from her eyes and blotting her shirt of excess liquid.

"You okay?" he asked a few minutes later, watching her closely.

Boy, was she making points with this guy, she thought. "What do you mean, we'll be living together?" she managed to croak through her raw throat.

He grinned again, which wasn't in the least fair. He truly had a killer smile that she found totally distracting. "Oh! Is that what startled you? Hey, I didn't mean anything by it. But since this is the only house on the island, you don't have much choice. But don't worry, there are a half dozen bedrooms, and we'll have Carmela and Romano here to chaperon us, if you're concerned about being in a compromising situation."

She attempted to gather her dignity, which was a little tough given her present circumstances. "I wasn't worried. I suppose I was hoping to get off the island before having to spend a night."

"Not a chance. Romano might be able to take you over to St. Thomas in the morning, but I'm not certain how that would help you reach your ship. Was that to be one of the stops?"

"On the way back, I think," she replied hollowly.

He held out his hand. "I'm Steve Antonelli, from L.A."

Robin looked at his hand and hesitantly placed hers into it. "Robin McAlister. Texas."

"Yeah, I'd already gotten the Texan part."

She raised her brows. "From?"

"The way you talk. I have a neighbor in my condo association who came from Texas. You sound a lot like her."

Robin tugged on her hand and he immediately let go.

"You said you wanted to contact your roommate. I'm surprised he wasn't with you on today's outing."

"My roommate is female and she wasn't interested in the tide pools." She looked down at her hands clenched in her lap. "I wish I'd been less eager to see them, as well."

"Let's go in the house, and I'll see what I can do about getting a phone number for you. That sound okay?"

She nodded.

He ushered her into a spacious living area with floor-to-ceiling windows on opposite walls. The view was spectacular. It felt as though they were outdoors. A gentle breeze wafted through the open windows. This was a truly beautiful place to stay.

"You have a fantastic home," she said, clutching her carryall to her chest and turning in a slow circle. She could see a dining area through an arched opening into one part of the house. On the fourth wall a hallway stretched into the distance, leading to another wing of the house.

"It belongs to a friend. I feel fortunate to be able to stay here."

"I can certainly understand that."

"If you'll excuse me, I'll get my phone. Just have a seat," he said and left the room.

She looked at the rattan furniture with its colorful, printed cushions and decided not to get sand and the sticky remains of her spilled drink on any of it. She took off her hat and carefully laid it on a nearby table.

When she glanced into the mirror above the table, she made a face. Her nose was glowing like Rudolph's, her braid had more wisps hanging out than were still in the braid, and her clothes were hopelessly damp and disreputable.

No wonder he was less than impressed with her. Wouldn't Cindi be dying laughing if she could witness this meeting! Robin would give most anything she could think of to have Cindi here with her. She would know just what to say and how to behave around Steve Antonelli from Los Angeles, California. Cindi's vivaciousness charmed everyone she met. Cindi didn't have a shy bone in her body, something that Robin had often envied about her.

Robin turned away from the mirror. She didn't need a reminder of what she looked like. A large seascape caught her eye, and she wandered over to look at it, before walking over to the window to enjoy the view.

She didn't hear Steve enter the room until he spoke. "Here you go. I have a ship's officer on the phone."

Robin gratefully took the phone, feeling as if she'd been offered a lifeline before she sank beneath the waves of inadequacy and shyness that had taken over. She explained who she was and what had happened and asked what she could do to get back on board the ship.

Her heart sank at the answer. After sending a message to Cindi, she thanked the ship's officer and ended the call. Steve had gone into the kitchen while she made the call, so she set the phone down on the glass table in front of the sofa, fighting tears. Of course she wasn't surprised that they weren't going to come back and pick her up. She realized they had a schedule to keep.

But until she had actually spoken to them, she hadn't wanted to face the fact that she was stranded here, stranded with a stranger who at best saw her as a nuisance.

When he walked back into the room, Steve was eating a piece of fruit. "Everything okay?" he asked.

She swallowed around the lump in her throat. "Well, not really."

"They can't pick you up?" he asked, with a hint of sympathy in his voice that almost caused her to lose what little control she had over the tears threatening to fall.

"No. They are on a very strict schedule. They suggested that I meet them in St. Thomas on their way back north." She realized what that meant. "That's five days from now." She glanced down at her bag. Five days. How was she going to manage for five days with no more than what she'd carried in her bag? She chewed on her lower lip. "You mentioned that someone could give me a ride to St. Thomas?"

He nodded. "Romano can take you whenever you need to go." He paused, as though searching for words. "I don't want to get too personal, but do you have any money with you?"

Oh, no! She had been so concerned about clothes that she hadn't even thought of a need for cash. She shook her head ruefully. "I'm afraid not. I left my purse and valuables on the ship. Do you suppose I could arrange to send him money once I get home?"

Steve cleared his throat, and his lips twitched, as though fighting a smile. "I wasn't thinking about Romano. He wouldn't charge you for the trip, because he goes over there on a regular basis. I was thinking about your attempting to stay in St. Thomas until the ship came back. Or getting a flight back home, rather than wait. Unless you can have money wired to you, I'm afraid you're going to be forced to stay here until time to meet your ship.''

He must think she was a real airhead. She hadn't gotten that far in her thinking. Of course he was right. Without money she was severely handicapped. She knew that she could call her parents and they would immediately arrange to have tickets and cash waiting for her. But that would mean she'd have to tell them what had happened to her.

She didn't want to do that. If they ever found out that she'd gotten herself stranded on an island in the Caribbean, her entire family would say her actions proved that she needed someone to look after her.

No. She would do almost anything rather than notify her parents, which meant staying here for the next few days.

"I, uh, would really prefer not to notify my parents. They would get upset, and it really isn't necessary to do that, if, uh, you don't mind my staying here.''

"Do you still live at home?'' he asked, his voice sounding a little strained.

"Actually, I'm in my last year of college at UT in Austin. My parents have a ranch a few hours west of there.''

"Ah, a college student. Is this your first cruise?''

She nodded. "And my last. I'd never realized I would feel so claustrophobic on board a ship that size.'' She sighed. "Except for all the trouble I'm causing you, I've got to admit that I much prefer being on solid ground.''

"You're not going to be any trouble."

"I'll stay out of your way. I promise. You won't even know I'm here."

He laughed, his teeth flashing white in his darkly tanned face. "Ms. McAlister, there's no way I'm not going to know you're here. In the first place, there's no reason for you to avoid me. I promise, you're perfectly safe with me."

"What do you do when you're not on vacation?" she asked, her curiosity outweighing her manners.

"I'm a cop."

Her eyes widened. "Really? How interesting. I don't believe I've ever met a policeman before."

"I promise not to bore you with stories. One of the reasons I'm here is to forget about all of that."

"I see. Then you've been a policeman a long time?"

"Long enough," he replied shortly. That was a subject he obviously didn't want to discuss, which was fine with her.

Robin wondered how old he was. He looked to be in his early thirties, probably at least ten years older than she was. Of course, there was nothing wrong with that. Her dad was ten years older than her mom and they had a great relationship.

Oh my gosh. Why did I think of that? There was no reason to think that this man could possibly be interested in her. His attitude toward her had been similar to the way her brother, Jason, treated her most of the time—an amused tolerance that made her wish she'd met him under other circumstances. She found him to be very attractive and hoped, since she was going to be staying here with him, that he might be attracted to her, as well.

Wouldn't her dad and brothers be screaming bloody

murder at the idea! That thought was enough to cheer her enormously.

"Why don't you let me show you to your room?" Steve said, and she realized she'd been lost in thought for several minutes. "I'm sure you'd like to shower and freshen up." He glanced at her bag. "Did you happen to bring anything else to wear?"

"A few things, but not much. I'd only planned to be away a few hours."

"I'll see what Carmela may be able to find for you. The owner's wife may have left some items here that could help out."

"I'd appreciate it."

He smiled and turned away. As she followed him down the hallway, he said, "Why don't you rest for a while? If you fall asleep, I'll wake you in time for dinner. You're in for a treat. Carmela is a wonderful cook. I hope you'll make yourself at home while you're here."

Her heart lightened. He really was being very gracious about all of this. Maybe everything would work out all right.

Four

Steve paused in the long hallway in front of one of the slatted doors, opened it and stepped aside. "I believe you'll find everything you need." He nodded toward her foot and ankle. "That looks like a nasty scrape. I'll bring you some antibiotic cream to put on it."

She glanced down in surprise. "Oh, with everything that's happened, I'd forgotten about my foot." She looked around the room. "Are you sure I should have this room? It's the master bedroom, isn't it?"

He shook his head. "Just one of the guest rooms. I'll go talk to Carmela about finding some extra clothes for you."

Steve closed the door and forced himself to walk, not run, away from this new predicament.

He really didn't mind having company for a few days, but the last type of visitor he needed was a schoolgirl with a face and body that could have easily graced the centerfold of a popular men's magazine and the innocent gaze of a fawn.

If Ray ever heard about this, he would be laughing his fool head off.

He found Carmela in the kitchen, preparing dinner. "I guess you figured out we're going to have an extra visitor for the next few days."

Carmela laughed. "It's good that you don't spend so much time alone. She's a very pretty girl."

"Well, yeah, actually I did happen to notice that." They both laughed, although he knew his laugh was a little hollow. "I was wondering if you know of any extra women's clothing around here. All she has is whatever she's carrying in that bag, which can't be much."

"I think I can find some things for her. She's taller than Mrs. Ed, but they both be slender. I'll go see what I can find for her."

"Thanks."

Next he went to the bathroom off his bedroom and found the antibiotic cream. He pretended not to notice that his heart rate hadn't slowed down much since he'd first spotted her on the beach. She was an unusually attractive woman, but it was her eyes that his thoughts kept remembering. Large, emerald-green and wide set, they were framed with dark, thick lashes and slightly tilted at the outer corners, with a trusting innocence shining from them that made his heart ache.

When she smiled, he saw a flash of dimples in her cheeks. She hadn't smiled much, but he could understand she was in a situation that would disturb the most seasoned traveler. She reminded him of a freshly hatched chick, bewildered by its surroundings and desperately trying not to show it.

He found it interesting that she didn't want to contact

her family. He wondered why. In fact, there were many intriguing questions that came to his mind where she was concerned.

He was going to enjoy getting to know her better.

Robin watched the door close behind Steve before she looked around at the room where she would be spending the next few days.

One wall had floor-to-ceiling windows with lush tropical plants on the other side of the glass, adding color and beauty to the room. Now she knew how Alice felt when she stepped through the looking glass.

She wished there were some way for her to speak to Cindi. She wanted to reassure her that things could be so much worse than they'd turned out. She could just imagine that Cindi had freaked when she'd discovered that Robin wasn't on the launch when it returned to the ship. Hopefully, she'd received word by now that Robin was safe and would meet up with them in a few days.

In the meantime she really wanted to get rinsed off.

Still carrying her bag, she opened one of the doors and discovered a huge, walk-in closet. Unfortunately it was empty of everything but clothes hangers. She closed that door and opened the next one. A large bathroom made up of large ceramic tiles and mirrors and brass fixtures awaited her. There was a glass-enclosed shower as well as an oversize tub with water jets.

She quickly unpacked her bag, shaking her head at the wrinkled condition of her slacks and the lack of any other clothes to wear. After she removed her shirt and shorts, she looked at the swimsuit she'd worn underneath and devoutly wished she'd worn underwear instead.

Robin turned on the shower and finished undressing, then brushed out her hair. There were bottles of shampoo

and conditioner sitting on the cabinet, she was relieved
to discover, as well as several kinds of bath soap.

She gathered them up and stepped beneath the wonderfully refreshing gush of water in the shower. She lathered and rinsed her hair, then worked conditioner through
it, before thoroughly soaping her body.

By the time Robin stepped out of the shower and
wrapped the luxurious towel around her body, she felt
much better. She towel dried her hair, combed the tangles
out and searched for a hair dryer. It was on the shelf
beneath the sink.

This was one of the few times when Robin was thankful for her naturally wavy hair. By the time she finished
drying it, her hair fell in waves around her face, neck and
shoulders.

She opened the door and went back into the bedroom.
Carmela must have visited while she was in the shower.
There was a stack of clothing on the bed as well as a
tube of antibiotic cream.

Still wrapped in the towel, she sat and propped her
foot on her other knee. The scrape on the outside of her
right foot and ankle no longer bled, but looked red and
angry. She uncapped the cream and took her time rubbing
it onto the wound. The cream felt soothing.

Afterward, she stood and sorted through the stack.

A caftan caught her eye, and she slipped it on. It was
a swirl of orange, gold and rust colors that blended well
with her hair color. The neckline was low and it was a
little short for her height but it would serve for now.

There were also some sleeveless T-shirts and some
well-washed shorts that she thought would fit. At the bottom was a sleep shirt made of soft cotton.

Meanwhile, she could have her own clothes laundered
and use them as a change, as well. She stretched out on

the bed, deciding to take Steve's advice and rest. Within minutes she was asleep.

Steve tapped on her door sometime later. He hadn't heard anything from her room in more than two hours. When she didn't respond he quietly opened the door and saw her asleep on the bed.

She looked like a sleeping princess in her flowing gown and her hair spread lustrously across her pillow. He stepped into the room and walked over to where she lay. Her skin looked silky smooth and a little gilded by the sun.

Seeing her like this made him realize what a precarious situation they were in. No red-blooded male could possibly ignore her beauty, but what drew him as a man racked with cold to a blazing fire was her freshness and her innocence. He had forgotten such a thing existed, which was another sign that he'd been working in the field too long.

The thin material of her caftan had slipped off her shoulder and exposed part of her breast. That's right. She'd been wearing a halter top—of a swimsuit, perhaps—when he first spotted her through his glasses. There was a strong chance she'd been wearing a bathing suit beneath her clothes instead of the usual panties and bra.

Just what he didn't need to think about. His young visitor was wearing nothing beneath her robe. He could see himself struggling not to think about that for the next few days.

"Robin?"

She stirred. "Hmm?"

"Dinner's ready. I figured you might be hungry by now."

Her eyes drifted open, and she stared at him blankly

for a moment before she suddenly sat up in bed. "Oh! I'm sorry. I didn't mean to fall asleep."

"No problem. I'll meet you in the dining room in a few minutes."

He did an about-face and strode out of the room before he followed the strong impulse he had to kiss the awakening beauty until she melted in his arms.

Robin stretched and yawned, feeling as though she could sleep through the rest of the afternoon and evening. She slid off the bed and took one of the shirts and one of the pairs of shorts to the bathroom. She dug into her carryall and pulled out the second bathing suit, which was a very skimpy bikini. It would have to serve as undergarments. She'd bought it on impulse, thinking she could use it to sunbathe, but hadn't actually had the nerve to do so. After fastening it, she looked in the mirror, her eyes widening.

The top was engineered in such a way that she looked much fuller, her breasts thrust upward and outward. It was very flattering to what she'd always considered her slight upper build. She stepped into the bottom that rode high on her hips, then finished dressing. After running her brush through her hair, she settled for a little lipstick, put on her shoes and left the bedroom.

She saw Steve in the dining room, lighting a pair of tall yellow tapers on a small table sitting in the bow window of the room. An arrangement of golden flowers curved around the base of the candles. Orange place mats with brightly colored pottery were arranged across from each other.

She paused in the archway, a little shaken by the idea that she would be dining so intimately with this gorgeous hunk. His dark skin glistened in the candlelight. A white sleeveless T-shirt was a stark contrast to his tan and thick, black hair. He had on a pair of snug khaki shorts that stopped midthigh, the clothes revealing his well-developed muscles in both arms and legs.

He wore a pair of thongs on his well-formed feet.

"This looks so enchanting, I'm not sure that I'm not still dreaming," she said.

He glanced up at the sound of her voice, then blew out the match. "If those are borrowed clothes, they certainly fit nicely," he said.

She could feel herself blushing. "Yes, they're borrowed. My others have had a rough day."

"If you'll give them to Carmela, she'll clean them for you."

"I hate to put her to any trouble."

"She won't think of it that way."

They spoke lightly, easily, as though they were old friends, Robin thought, but the undercurrent of knowing they were strangers sharing a house caused a tension to creep into the room.

"Here," he said, drawing out her chair, "have a seat."

The dining alcove overlooked the patio area. A slow-moving fan stirred the air above the table. Chilled wine rested in a bucket of ice, and a sliced assortment of colorful fruit was artistically displayed in a bowl. Broiled fish and rice pilaf filled each large plate.

"Wow," she breathed. "Do you eat like this every meal?"

He grinned. "Yes, as a matter of fact, I do. Carmela is a wonder. She's the best-kept secret the owner has. She could make a fortune working as a chef in the States."

Once Steve sat across from her, he filled their wine-glasses and filled their salad bowls.

They ate for a while in silence. Robin hadn't realized

how hungry she was until she started eating. She darted glances across the table from time to time, admiring her companion, making mental notes for a future time when all of this would seem like some fantasy she'd made up.

Steve cleared his throat and said, ''As long as we're going to be here together, we might as well get acquainted, don't you think?''

She smiled. ''All right.''

When she didn't say anything more, he laughed. ''Why don't you go first? What are your plans when you get out of college?''

''I've been working with a public relations firm in Austin the past two summers, and they've offered me a position there. I've also been considering applying for a similar situation with one of the national hotel chains—planning and arranging for conferences, and that sort of thing.'' She took a sip of wine. ''How about you? What are your duties at work?''

''I work homicide.''

''Really? I would guess that's a very rough assignment.''

He nodded. ''It can be. You can burn out in a hurry. I hadn't realized how close I was until I actually arrived here. I couldn't stop my mind from racing. Of course by the time I reached the place, I'd been traveling so long I was really jet lagged. Now it's hard for me to think about the life I have in California.''

''Do you have any family?'' she asked, already aware that he didn't wear a ring.

''My parents live in Santa Barbara, a couple of hours away. I was an only child for a long time. My sister, Tricia, was born when I was eleven, then Scott came along a couple of years later. The twins, Todd and Greg, were born three years after that.''

"So you have three brothers!" she said with a laugh. "Well, we have that in common, at least. I always wished for a sister, but Mom said I'd have to settle for Cindi, who is as close as a sister could be."

"I was away in college by the time the twins got out of the baby stage, so it's hard to think of them as brothers."

Carmela came and cleared the table before bringing them dessert and coffee. Steve caught a twinkle in her eyes when she saw them chatting so amiably together.

What could he say? This certainly wasn't the toughest assignment he'd ever had, entertaining a charming young lady.

"What about your family?" he asked.

"My dad owns a ranch, as I think I mentioned earlier. I have two older brothers and one younger. I'm very close to my mom. People often mistake us for sisters. She was a highly paid New York model before they started their family."

"I must admit that when I first spotted you on the beach I wondered if you were a model."

Her eyes sparkled, and she flashed her dimpled grin. "Oh! Well, thank you! I'd definitely take that as a compliment."

He lifted his wineglass in a salute and said, "Just as it was meant." He took a sip. "Are you close to your brothers?"

"Closer than I'd like at times," she replied ruefully. "Don't get me wrong. I have a very warm, loving family," she said, taking a bite of pie. "The problem is that sometimes they're a little *too* loving. My brothers seem to think I'm helpless without them to look after me. I can just imagine what they would say if they ever heard about my being marooned on an island."

"Ah. So that's why you don't want to call home for help," he said, leaning back in his chair with a smile.

"Exactly. I'm embarrassed enough that this happened without letting them know about it. They'd never let me hear the end of it. I really think I would have made it back in time if I hadn't fallen." She glanced down at her foot. "I guess I should consider myself lucky I didn't sprain my ankle...or worse." When she looked back at him she was unnerved by the glow in his eyes. There was something about the way he looked at her that made her feel all quivery inside. She said the first thing that came to mind.

"How long have you been a policeman?"

"I graduated from the academy eight years ago. I've been a homicide detective for the past three years."

"Was your dad a policeman, as well?"

Steve shook his head. "My dad played baseball for Atlanta years ago. He retired when I was fifteen."

"I'm afraid I don't know much about sports, especially baseball. My brothers are all football fans, so being around them and listening to them taught me a little about that sport, but not much. Did you play sports growing up?"

"As a matter of fact, I did. I planned to play baseball professionally until my junior year in college when an injury to my arm knocked me out of any hopes of making it to the big league." Before she could say anything, he went on. "The man who owns this island, Ed Kowolski, played on the same team as my dad. They were close friends and roommates on the road. I've always considered Ed more of an uncle than just a friend of the family." He looked at her glass. "More wine?"

"Oh, no, thank you. I'm not much of a drinker." She glanced out the window. "Oh, look, the sun is going down. With the clouds on the horizon, the sunset is going to be spectacular.''

Steve stood. "I know of a great place to view the sunset. You want to see it?"

"Sure," she said. He held out his hand to her. It was such a natural gesture that she thought nothing of taking it, until she felt his warm palm pressed against hers. There was an electrical surge that shot through her body as though she'd been zapped by lightning.

Her hand jerked, but he didn't seem to notice.

He led her outside, then over a path that ended at a wooden bench seat facing west. The sun was rapidly sinking into the ocean, turning the water a fiery red, and the sky became an artist's palette of colors.

No matter how often he saw it, Steve was transfixed by the spectacle. He seldom noticed the sun when he was in L.A. Working the evening shift, he rarely thought about anything but work at that time of day.

Or any other time of day, for that matter. Yet now, here he was, taking in the daily spectacular of light and color with an extremely attractive young woman. If Ray could see him now, he'd definitely agree that Steve's vacation was going better than his most extravagant expectations.

He also noticed that she seemed as spellbound as he was by the sight. He appreciated her silence as they sat there until night had fallen and the stars took over the sky.

Finally she straightened and sighed. "No wonder you enjoy being here so much."

"Yeah. It's definitely a soothing experience."

She stood. "I appreciate your hospitality, but I don't want to take up any more of your time, so I think I'll go on to bed."

"You can't be serious. It's much too early to sleep, especially after that nap you had earlier. How about a game of pool? Or maybe some cards. Do you like to play?"

He could barely see her face in the shadows. She stood facing him, her hands clasped behind her back. "Are you sure?" she asked. "You've been more than generous with your time. I don't want to become a nuisance."

Steve realized that he was thoroughly enjoying her company. The hours had slipped away since he'd found her. Now that she was here, he didn't want to spend any more time alone. He wanted to show her the island, take her with him to explore the parts he hadn't seen yet.

All of that would have to take place when the sun was up. But for now...

"You aren't a nuisance. I promise. I'm sorry if I sounded like a grump earlier today. Let's go back to the house and I'll show you the game room." He laughed. "In fact, now that you're here, I'll have someone to compete against. Most of those games take two people."

They returned to the house. He took her upper arm to guide her along the way. He liked touching her. He rubbed his thumb along her skin, enjoying the silky feel of it.

She shivered.

"I should have brought you a jacket," he said, draping his arm across her shoulders and pulling her close to his side. She was a nice fit. A perfect fit, actually.

"I didn't realize there was a pool table," she said, sounding a little breathless. He was feeling a little breathless himself.

"Yep. Do you like to play?" he asked, hoping she couldn't hear the rapid beating of his heart.

"Sure." They reached the terrace, and he opened the

sliding door for her. Carmela had left one of the lamps on for them and had gone home to Romano for the night. They were alone in the house.

Not that it mattered, Steve thought. He'd meant what he'd told her. She was perfectly safe with him. If he said it often enough, he was certain he'd be able to convince himself.

"Have you played much pool?" he asked, leading the way to the game room.

She chuckled, and he glanced over his shoulder. "Whenever my brothers would let me play. I've always enjoyed the game, though."

He'd nodded. He would go easy on her. There was no reason to embarrass her. After all, tonight the game would be more a form of recreation than the way he and Ray liked to play—competitive and cutthroat.

He stepped back at the doorway and said, "Go ahead."

The large game room had a pool table, table tennis, an octagonal-shaped card table and various games, dice and assorted poker chips on display. "You can break."

"But shouldn't we—"

He waved his hand in a dismissive gesture. "No need. You go ahead."

She shrugged and said, "Well, okay, but that doesn't seem fair to me."

What a nice attitude, he thought. She didn't want to take advantage of him. If she only knew that he'd spent more of his time in college shooting pool than he had studying. Not that he would ever let her know just how well he could play. He certainly didn't want to intimidate her.

So Steve watched as Robin racked the balls into a tight fit, lined up the cue and shot, putting two in, one stripe and one solid. She studied the table. "I'll take solid," she said.

He looked the table over and agreed with her choice. At least she understood the game. Her break had been good—she had a long, clean stroke—and she'd lucked out putting two balls into pockets on that first hit.

After she cleared the table of solids and gracefully sank the eight ball, she turned to him apologetically and said, "I'm sorry. You didn't get a chance to shoot."

He laughed. "Don't apologize. You did wonderfully well. Go ahead. You break again."

"Well, I know that's the rules, but don't you want to take your turn?"

"Don't worry about it. I'll get my chance soon enough."

By the time he got that chance, she'd cleared the table twice more and had only two balls left on the table for the fourth game. All right, she was better than good. She had a steady hand, a good eye and great form, and if she'd had any idea of his condescending attitude toward her when they'd first started, he'd be feeling humiliated by now. Instead, he was having trouble keeping his attention on the game.

She seemed totally unconscious of how she looked stretched across the table, her long legs making it easier for her to handle some of the more awkward shots.

"How did you say you learned to play?" he finally asked, his curiosity getting the better of him.

"My dad taught me."

"Ah."

Steve reminded himself not to challenge her father, should they ever meet, to a game of pool, if the student was any indication of the teacher's skills.

He lost track of time, determined to catch up with her.

He'd never seen a woman play with such concentrated skill. He was used to playing with women who were more experienced at gaining attention than placing shots. When Robin played, she seemed to be unaware of anything else but the angle of her next placement.

Only later did he realize that they'd spoken very little the entire evening. At one point he went to the kitchen and brought back a beer for him, a fruit punch drink for her. When she finally smiled and said, "I really need to get some sleep, Steve," he was astounded to discover that it was after one o'clock in the morning.

"You're three games ahead of me," he said ruefully. "You're good. You know that?"

She grinned. "Thanks. I had to learn to be good to keep up with my brothers."

Of course.

"And you're maybe a little bit competitive," he added with a grin.

She laughed. "I've been accused of such a thing on one or two occasions."

"I just bet you have."

They returned to the living room. "Well," she said a little uncertainly, "I guess I'll see you in the morning."

"Say, would you like to meet me on the beach at dawn, go for a morning swim? It's a great way to start the day."

"I'm not sure I'll be awake at that time."

"Oh. Well then, I'll see you when you get up. There's no hurry, of course. No time clocks to punch on this island, that's for sure." There was a forced heartiness to his voice that irritated him, but he couldn't seem to rid himself of it. He was feeling tense and more than a little irritable. Could it really have bothered him that she had beaten him so consistently? Surely not.

The only other thing that might be bothering him was the fact that he'd been in a semiaroused state for most of the evening. He was thankful she seemed to be oblivious of him.

Then again, that might be part of his problem. Let's face it, he wasn't used to being ignored. Didn't she feel the vibration that seemed to hum around them? He hadn't been able to keep his eyes off her all night.

"Well," she said with a hint of a smile, "I'll see you in the morning."

"Sure," he said. He needed to go to bed, too. Instead, he headed for the kitchen and another beer. What was the matter with him, anyway? He was acting as though he'd been rejected because she didn't want to stay up with him longer.

His problem was that most women he spent the evening with took for granted that they would be spending the night together, as well. So there was always that anticipation as the evening progressed—the long looks, the accidental touches that were intentional, maybe a teasing kiss or two.

But this situation was different. This hadn't been a date. She hadn't chosen to spend the time with him. He was her host and as such had to remember that she was here because she had no other place to stay.

He wandered off to bed, trying to figure out what was wrong with him. He'd been perfectly content to be here on his own, his meals magically appearing at specified times of the day.

Now he was having trouble planning to get up alone in the morning for his usual ritual of greeting the sun on the beach. He shook his head in disbelief before taking his shower. Eventually he sprawled out on his bed with a sigh. He'd feel more himself after a good night's sleep.

* * *

Robin came awake with a jolt and realized that she'd been dreaming—nightmarish dreams where she kept running to catch a train but always missed it. It didn't take much thought to figure out why she'd be having dreams about being left behind.

She rolled over with a groan, unwilling to go back to sleep if she was going to continue with that kind of dream pattern. She wondered what time it was. The owner obviously had chosen not to have clocks around the place.

She'd left her watch on the ship, not wanting to take a chance on getting sand or salt water into the gift her parents had given her for her high school graduation.

She sat up, running her hand through her hair.

Even though the room was dark, she was wide awake. She tossed back the sheet and went into the bathroom. Maybe she'd get dressed and go get something to drink in the kitchen. Surely Carmela had a clock in there.

After slipping into the clothes she'd worn last night, Robin quietly opened her door and listened, but heard nothing stirring. She had no idea where Steve slept.

The hallway was dark, but there was a faint light coming through the windows in the living room. She felt her way down the long expanse until she reached the lighter area where she finally relaxed. Only then did she realize she'd been holding her breath.

She shook her head in disgust. This wasn't some kind of gothic movie where a gruesome being might jump out at her at any moment.

Now that she was in the living room, she had no trouble finding her way into the kitchen. She flipped on the light, blinking until her eyes adjusted. Ah. There was a clock on the stove. She peered at the hands. It was almost six o'clock.

She poured herself some fresh fruit juice from the refrigerator and looked around. There was fruit as well as fresh rolls. She took a bite of mango, then wiped the juice that ran down her chin with the back of her hand.

Robin wandered over to the window and looked out. There was a little more light than when she'd first looked outside. She could see the water, washing up on the shore in rhythmic waves, leaving a white wreath of foam decorating the sand.

She finished her juice, picked up her mango, then went to the sliding doors and let herself outside. The stars were still clear, but there was a faint lightening of the sky to the east.

After following the path to the shore, she walked along the shallows, looking out over the blackness that was the ocean.

Her thoughts went back to the restless night she'd just spent. She'd kept waking up with a jolt, wondering where she was, wondering why she was alone, wishing that Cindi were there.

This wouldn't be a bad situation if her friend were here making jokes about their getting themselves into such a situation. Cindi had a lighthearted way of looking at life. Robin envied her the ability. She knew she took everything too seriously, but so far, acknowledging the flaw hadn't helped her to overcome the tendency.

Well, now she had a chance to practice seeing the humor in the situation she'd gotten herself in.

The fact was the early-morning view was becoming spectacular. She paused and looked to the east. The sky was rapidly turning colors, from the dark blue-black of the night to softer pastel colors. A line of low-hanging clouds on the horizon suddenly burst into bright red as though catching fire.

She finished her mango and tossed the seed into the water, leaned over and washed her hands in the surf, splashing water onto her face, as well. Then she retreated to the softer, dry sand and sat down, prepared to watch nature's spectacular display of light and color.

There was no sense of time passing as the sun suddenly appeared at the edge of the horizon, then rapidly moved until it seemed to balance like a bright orange ball on the line where the ocean met the sky.

She sighed. Her petty concerns seemed to dissipate and disappear with the light breeze that flirtatiously brushed against her cheek before dancing away.

Eventually she got up, dusted the sand from the seat of her shorts and started back down the beach the way she had come. When she reached the area where the path led back to the house, she noticed a towel and thongs lying on the sand. She raised her hand to shield her eyes from the sun and peered out to the water.

Eventually she spotted Steve as he energetically swam parallel to the beach. He was far enough out that all she could see of him was his dark head and an occasional flash of his arms as he moved through the water.

Robin unbuttoned her shirt and unfastened her shorts, tossing the items aside. She had her swimsuit beneath, the one she was using for underwear, but it was still swimming attire.

The water felt silky smooth against her feet and ankles and unbelievably warm. She ran through the shallows and launched herself into swimming mode when the water reached her waist.

She'd forgotten about her hair. She dived under the water and came up face first, then gathered her hair into three sections and quickly braided it, tying it off with a part of her hair, then tossing it over her shoulder and swimming once more.

She made no attempt to go out as far as Steve, but was content to swim at a leisurely pace, making certain she didn't drift too far away from shore. The sun kissed her face and shoulders as she moved steadily through the water, a smile on her face. This was quite a nice way to start the day, she had to admit.

When Steve first spotted her, he had to look again to make sure he wasn't seeing a mermaid. So she had managed to wake up early enough to enjoy an early-morning swim, after all.

He swam to the shallows, then stood, wading the rest of the way until he left the water behind and reached his towel. Shaking the sand from the towel, he rubbed it over his head and face before quickly swiping it across his body. Then he sat down and waited for his houseguest to finish her swim.

He leaned back on his elbows and watched as she moved lazily along in the water as though savoring the feel of it against her skin. A ripple of awareness slid over him. He would guess that she was sexually inexperienced, because she seemed to be so unaware of her own sexuality, but he realized that she was a very sensuous person. He wondered how she could have reached this age and not be more aware of her effect on the male of the species.

When she became tired, she stopped swimming and stood, waist-deep, looking out at the ocean, her back to him. She'd braided her hair, and it now hung in a long rope down the middle of her back.

He stared for a moment in shock, wondering if she was wearing anything. Then he saw the flesh-toned strap that went around her back. Wow. For a minute there he had actually wondered if she had chosen to swim nude.

Then she turned and started toward him, and he had to take a deep breath because not only was the suit flesh-colored but there wasn't much of it. A triangle covered the area at the apex of her thighs, and two other triangles covered her chest.

Hell, she could have started a riot on a public beach. Didn't she know better than to— He lost his train of thought as he took in the picture she made coming out of the water.

She walked with an unconscious grace, her hips swinging slightly in an undulating rhythm that had his heart racing. Her long legs seemed to go on forever.

Steve closed his eyes and recited all the many reasons why it wouldn't be a good idea to stare at his visitor with obvious hunger in his eyes.

"Hi!" she said. "I forgot to bring a towel. May I use yours?"

He nodded, then squinted up at her, hoping she thought it was the sun that kept his eyes nearly closed as he handed her the towel. Backlit as she was, she glowed. There was no other word for it.

"Thanks." After a long moment he heard the rustle of clothes and opened one eye. She was stepping into a pair of shorts he hadn't noticed lying nearby, then she pulled on her shirt. He sat up.

"Refreshing, isn't it?" he said, his voice still sounding as if he'd swallowed a frog.

"Oh, yes. I don't remember ever enjoying the beach more than this morning. There's something magical about this place," she said.

He nodded. "Yeah, I've been thinking the same thing.

I've been up every morning I've been here to see the sun rise and to start my day with a swim. Nothing like it.''

''You're very fortunate to have a place like this to come to.''

''Yes, that's true. I don't know about you,'' he said, glancing at the sun, ''but I'm ready for some breakfast.''

''Sounds good.'' She held out her hand to him and he grasped it, then allowed her to pull him to his feet. His hand tingled, and as soon as he was upright, he casually let go of her hand.

''I have some suggestions on how we can spend the day,'' he said, motioning her ahead of him on the trail back to the house.

''Please don't feel that you have to entertain me. I noticed that the owners have several novels in their bookcases that I haven't had a chance to read.''

''You can read anytime, but how many chances do you get to explore your very own island?'' He reached around and pushed the door open, then allowed her to step inside the house.

She turned and laughed up at him. Oh, those dimples were something else. More than a little distracting, to be sure. ''Well, when you put it that way, how can I resist? Whatever you want to do is fine with me,'' she said.

She looked unbelievably young standing in the early-morning sunlight, without a hint of makeup to mar her natural beauty. Steve had a sudden presentiment that he might be the one way over his head here. He was reacting to this woman in a way he'd never reacted to a woman before.

It scared him. But he refused to back off. Nothing that they started here could go anywhere, anyway. They lived half a country apart, and long-distance relationships never worked.

So why shouldn't he explore this attraction between them? If she was willing, maybe there was a chance they could have a wonderful few days together. Once they established the ground rules, maybe understood each other better, there was a chance they could enjoy a romantic holiday for them both to remember.

Five

Steve stared out at the night from his bedroom window.

Three days had passed since Robin had shown up, and she had managed to turn his life into a spinning top. She had just spent the evening soundly beating him at poker. And why not? Granted she was a hell of a poker player, but his brain refused to focus on anything so mundane as red and black marks on random cards.

Being around her was rapidly turning him into a raving lunatic.

Therefore, he'd chosen to retreat to his bedroom on the pretext that he was worn out from their strenuous day. So here he was trying to figure out what to do about his fascination with the woman.

When he'd awakened early that morning, he'd decided that a day of strenuous exercise would help him ignore his increasing attraction to her. With that in mind, he'd suggested a hike to the center of the island, where he'd previously found a pool with a waterfall, thinking that she would enjoy seeing it. By the time he realized how seductive the place was, it was too late to change his plans.

No matter how he'd fought the memories since their return, they continued to flood over him....

Perspiration trickled down his cheek, and Steve paused to wipe it away with his forearm. When he'd started out to find the fall and pool a few hours ago, he'd forgotten about the steep climb into the interior of the island as well as the increased heat, once a person moved away from the breeze coming off the ocean.

He held out his hand to Robin. "I'd forgotten how hot it is at this time of day."

She took his hand and allowed him to help her the rest of the way up the path to where he stood. "You promised the climb would be worth it," she reminded him. She took off her wide-brimmed hat and waved it in front of her like a fan. They were both breathing hard from the exertion of the climb.

"I stick with that promise. In fact, I think we're almost there. At least the rest of the way is on fairly level ground."

She looked through the fronds toward the ocean. "I still haven't grown used to the different colors of the ocean. It's constantly changing, have you noticed? I had no idea a body of water could be so fascinating."

"I know what you mean," he replied. "I live near the Pacific and since coming here I've realized that I don't spend enough of my time just enjoying it. I've already made several promises to myself about how I'm going to change my routine once I'm home. A trip to the beach is going to be part of my weekly agenda from now on."

He was pleased that his voice sounded casual and even, and since she faced away from him, he didn't have to hide the expression on his face as he enjoyed the sight of her standing there unaware of anything but the view.

She wore her shorts and shirt over a swimsuit, with the shirt unbuttoned and hanging open. He enjoyed watching the way she moved—with an unconscious grace that stirred his heart. She was as graceful as a gazelle. He couldn't believe he was waxing poetic over this woman, but she had certainly managed to infiltrate all his defenses during these past few days.

She was a good sport, willing to try new things without fear of looking foolish. He liked to tease her just to see her blush. Her eyes mesmerized him, with their shadows and light. There were times when the sea was the exact shade of green as her eyes.

He forced himself to turn away and continued following the route he'd marked the first time he came up this way. He heard the falls before he saw them and looked around at her. "I hear them. We're almost there."

"Not too soon for me, that's for sure. I think I could just stand under the water for the next several hours without complaining," Robin replied.

They stepped through the fronds that surrounded the inviting pool. The mist from the waterfall wafted over them.

"Oh, this is too perfect," Robin exclaimed with a laugh, throwing her arms wide as though to embrace the scene. She reached down and pulled off her shoes, then removed her shirt and shorts. "It looks like something from a movie set."

Steve stripped down to his swimsuit and stepped out of his shoes while he watched Robin slip into the water.

She gave a sigh of pleasure and swam toward the waterfall.

"How much exploring did you do when you were here before?" she asked, rolling over onto her back and floating. The clear water gave him a full view of her delectable body.

"I checked to make sure there wasn't anything in the water that could be considered harmful, if that's what you're asking," he replied, amused by the question.

"Oops. Maybe I should have asked before I got in. I was wondering if you'd actually gotten into the water before."

He grinned. "Don't worry. I wouldn't have brought you here if I thought you could get injured."

She groaned. "Now you sound like one of my brothers. Believe me, I have enough brothers, Steve. You don't need to join the crowd."

He lowered himself into the water and swam to her. When he stood, the water was to his neck. "You don't have to worry, Robin," he said, "I certainly don't think of you as my sister."

She lowered her feet, but continued to swim in place. They were facing each other with about a foot of water between them. She looked relaxed and happy, her skin glowing, her hair in its usual braid. "I'm almost afraid to ask how you think of me," she said, with a definite hint of shyness in her voice.

He reached out and encircled her waist and slowly brought her closer to him. "Do you really want to know?" he asked quietly, his hands resting lightly at her waist to keep her afloat. Otherwise, she would be fighting to keep her nose above the water.

Instead of pulling away from him, she placed her hands

on his shoulders, and stared deeply into his eyes. "Uh-huh."

"I think of you as beautiful, intelligent, sensitive, caring, and so sexy I can hardly keep my hands off you," he muttered.

Her gaze held his, although a delicious blush reddened her cheeks. "You think I'm sexy? Really?" She sounded astonished.

"You'd better believe it. And if I wasn't such a gentleman, I would have kissed you that very first night when you beat me so soundly at pool."

She pulled herself closer to him, until her breasts touched his chest and let her legs brush against his. "Are you feeling gentlemanly at the moment?" she asked with a mischievous grin.

"No, ma'am, I'm not."

"Good," she said with a smile. She pressed her lips lightly against his, as though daring him to respond. Or perhaps she was daring him *not* to respond, but he was flesh and blood, and no healthy male would have been able to resist her provocative invitation.

Her mouth trembled against his, mutely telling him she wasn't nearly so bold as she might wish him to believe. He didn't want to scare her—that was the very last thing he wanted to happen—so he returned the kiss with a light pressure, allowing her to take the lead.

She floated closer, entwining her legs with his. It was a good thing he was standing, because if he'd been treading water at that moment, they would both have gone under. Her utter trust in him scared him to death. They both needed to be on guard, here. He couldn't do this alone.

That's when he realized that her kiss was eager yet untutored, brushing against his mouth as though unsure of what to do next. He coaxed her mouth open and darted his tongue into the opening, lightly teasing, allowing her to guide him as to how far she wanted to go with this.

When she drew away, he released his hold on her and warily watched her expression as she gazed at him in surprise. Those long lashes fluttered closed and she leaned toward him once again, repeating the kiss, this time imitating his movements, her tongue toying with his, tracing the shape of his mouth before settling against him in a heated kiss that shot his temperature up to broil.

"Mmm," she said dreamily, slowly moving away from him. "That was even better than I could have hoped." Then she sank into the water until she was underwater and swam toward the waterfall.

Steve felt his body temperature had gone up enough to cause the water to boil around him. He wanted to pursue her, to indulge in more kisses that would eventually lead to...

He didn't want to think where it might lead. She hadn't given any indication that she wanted anything more from him than a light flirtation.

So he watched and waited throughout the afternoon for some sign of what she might want from him.

The kiss was never mentioned. Instead, they played in the water until he told her they needed to head back to the house. They dried off and pulled on their clothes over their wet suits, and Robin chatted with him on the way back as though nothing had happened.

There was no way she could not have been aware of his physical reaction to her, but she had ignored it.

If she was sending any signals, he wasn't reading them. Could she be so innocent as to not understand how badly he'd wanted to make love to her? She's treated the kiss as something casual between friends. Maybe that's

the way she saw them, new friends getting better acquainted.

What startled Steve was the realization that he wanted
more than friendship with Robin....

While they played poker later that night, Steve acknowledged to himself that he was in serious trouble.
Never having been in love, he wasn't certain of the symp-
toms, but he knew something strange was happening to
him.

As she systematically cleaned out his supply of poker
chips, all he could do was watch her expressions, study
the way wisps of hair framed her shell-like ears, marvel
at the length and thickness of her eyelashes—in short,
make a complete fool of himself.

If any of the men with whom he played poker on Tues-
day nights learned that he'd been soundly beaten by a
slip of a woman—an innocent college student—he'd become the laughing stock of the station. The bewildering
part to him was that he didn't care. That's when he knew
he had to come to grips with what was happening to him.
And more importantly, he had to decide what the hell he
was going to do about it.

Robin was too keyed-up to go to bed. After Steve ex-
cused himself for the night, she decided to walk out to
the wooden bench located near the rocky point where
they sat each evening to watch the sun go down. Now
there was little light except for the sliver of moon and a
sky full of stars. She sat and looked out at the water, the
foam along the top of the waves giving definition to the
movement of the sea.

She couldn't get their kiss out of her head. No doubt
he had a great deal of experience with that sort of thing,
but the heat they generated had blown Robin away. She

had wanted so much more, but didn't have a clue how to let him know.

He seemed to enjoy the kiss. At least he hadn't pushed her away. Of course most guys wouldn't turn down a kiss if it were offered. But he hadn't really taken her seriously, she could tell. He had teased her, keeping his hands firmly on her waist. She would have expected him to touch her more, maybe stroke her back or cup her breast, but he had done none of those things.

He'd said that he found her sexy, but maybe he'd said that to be polite. If he'd found her attractive, wouldn't he have kissed her again, maybe a simple good-night kiss?

She couldn't figure men out, that was for sure. Tonight he'd been so uninterested in their poker game that he'd paid little attention to the game and had allowed her to win most of the time. Was he bored with her being there? She still had two more days on the island. If he was bored trying to entertain her, that would explain why he'd gone to his room so early in the evening.

If only she knew how to let him know how attracted she was to him. What woman wouldn't be? He was probably used to women throwing themselves at him. The last thing she wanted to do was to make him uncomfortable by becoming a nuisance to him. He'd spent the past three days showing her the island, taking her swimming, playing cards, shooting pool. Now that she really thought about it, she could see where he might be impatient to get her off the island so he could have his privacy back.

She pulled her knees to her chest and wrapped her arms around her legs. Boy, she was a complete washout when it came to attracting a man who appealed to her. She'd hoped that by kissing him today he would get the message that she was turned on by him. Maybe he'd gotten the message, but just wasn't interested.

She sighed, wishing she knew what she could do or say to ease the tension between them. It was embarrassing to admit, even to herself, that she didn't have a clue how to woo a man into making love with her.

There. She'd faced it. That's what she wanted to have happen on this idyllic island vacation of hers. She wanted to be able to experience what her friends were all talking about. She'd never had a steady, so she hadn't been able to experiment in high school as Cindi and a few of her friends had.

She hadn't made out in the back seat of somebody's car. She really hated the fact that she had so little experience to draw on. As well as she knew her brothers, they had made certain that she didn't understand what turned a guy on, what made him want to make love. To hear them tell it, it didn't take much, which was why they never let her be alone with a date, always making certain that any double date she was on was properly supervised.

How ironic that she now had not only the perfect opportunity but the perfect dreamboat of a male, as well, and after kissing him and letting him know she was interested, he chose to go to bed early!

She propped her chin on her knees and stared out to sea. Slowly the majestic expanse of water and the soft sighs of the waves soothed her troubled mind and she allowed her thoughts to drift in the peace of the moment. When she finally roused herself to go inside, she was ready for sleep.

She'd also decided what she had to do to give Steve back his solitude.

Robin woke early the next morning—long before dawn—dressed and slipped into the kitchen for some food supplies. She left a note for Steve on the kitchen table, telling him that she would be gone for the day exploring the tide pools and sunbathing, and that she would see him that night.

By the time the sun appeared, she had walked the length of the island to the area where the tide pools were abundant. She spread her towel in the shade of one of the trees and stretched out to rest. She'd had another restless night and now the warm rays of the sun were soothing. She might take a short nap, then eat something before going exploring. She refused to feel sorry for herself. She'd had a wonderful time on the island.

As she drifted off to sleep, Robin smiled. She knew that she would never forget getting marooned on a tropical island and the man she had come to know there.

Steve took his usual swim that morning and was disappointed when it became clear that Robin wasn't going to join him as she had each morning since she'd arrived on the island. By the time he returned to the house, he was already eager to find her and share some of his ideas for the day's entertainment.

But first he showered and dressed in his usual uniform—shorts and swimsuit—before he wandered into the kitchen for something to eat. Carmela had coffee made as well as breakfast pastries and fruit sitting out.

She turned when he walked in and smiled at him. "You have a message," she said, pointing to the table.

Puzzled, Steve picked up a handwritten note and silently read:

Steve, you've been a wonderful host these past few days. I don't want to wear out my welcome. I've gone to the other end of the island for the day to give you back your solitude. I'll see you at sunset. Enjoy your day! Robin.

"Did you talk to her this morning?" he asked Carmela after reading the note.

"No, sir. I never saw her. She must have been up early. She made some sandwiches, took some bottled water and fruit, so I figure she's planning to be away for a while."

He poured himself a cup of coffee and munched on a lighter-than-air pastry. So. She was gone. He wondered what he'd done to offend her that she would choose to be gone her last full day on the island.

The only thing that came to mind was his retiring so early last night. She must have taken that to mean that he didn't want to spend any more time with her. Now *that* was almost amusing, given his actual state of mind.

Steve sighed, poured himself another cup of coffee and looked at his options. The safest thing he could do would be to leave her at the other end of the island. After all, she'd chosen to spend the day away from him. They'd managed to keep it light and fairly platonic, if he ignored that heated kiss yesterday, and being separated today made a great deal of sense.

She would leave the island tomorrow as planned, after which he'd never see her again.

No big deal, really. He'd forget all about her when his life returned to normal after his vacation ended.

No doubt that was the best resolution of their situation for all concerned.

The only problem with that was he didn't think his life would ever be the way it was before she'd shown up on the island. In her particular case, out of sight did not necessarily mean out of mind.

He'd never believed in long-distance romances, but he was willing to make an exception in this case. And he didn't want to waste this last day with an island between them. What he needed to do was to go find her, apologize

for his moodiness and make certain that she understood
he wanted to consider a long-term relationship with her.

As soon as he finished eating, Steve set off to the other
end of the island. He noticed clouds forming on the horizon, a sure sign that they were going to have rain
squalls later in the day. He felt confident that Robin
would not want to be out in that kind of weather, so he
was actually doing her a favor, warning her of a change
in the weather.

He had a proprietary feeling toward her that made him
uneasy, as though she were his to look after and care for.
That certainly wasn't the politically correct attitude for a
male to have in this day and time. At least he had sense
enough not to let on that he felt that way. He'd already
heard enough about her attitude toward her brothers to
know she'd be less than pleased with him.

He spotted her near where she'd been the first day.
He'd forgotten how far it was and had become concerned
that he may have missed her somehow when he rounded
a curve of the beach and saw her.

She lay near the trees that formed a dividing line between the lush vegetation and white sands. When he ap-
proached her he saw that she was sound asleep, her head
resting on her arm.

He felt like the prince discovering Sleeping Beauty.

He sank to his knees beside her and softly stroked her
cheek. "Robin?" he whispered, not wanting to startle
her.

She stirred, her long lashes fluttering before they revealed the soft-green of her eyes, still dazed with sleep.
She saw him and smiled sleepily up at him before her
lashes fluttered closed, as though her eyelids were too
heavy for her to hold open at the moment.

He stretched out beside her, propping himself on his

elbow, then leaned over and brushed her lips with his own. She tasted so good, and her lips were as delectably soft as he remembered them to be. He pulled back just as her eyes opened once again, so that they were inches away from each other.

"That was nice," she whispered. "I do like the way you kiss."

"That's good news because I thoroughly enjoy kissing you." To prove his point, he kissed her again, his mouth lingering on hers.

She touched his face with her long, slender fingers. "What are you doing here?" she asked, when he forced himself to draw away.

"I missed you," he replied simply.

"Really?" She sounded surprised.

"I'm sorry about last night," he said, pressing featherlight kisses on her cheek and the side of her neck. "I must have seemed very rude, leaving so early." As though unable to resist, he found her mouth once again.

By the time they both paused for much-needed air, they were trembling.

"I thought you were bored with me," she managed to say.

"Actually, I was having a huge fight with my better nature, who kept reminding me that you are very young and inexperienced and you need to become involved with someone your own age."

"I see." She traced the shape of his mouth with her fingertip. "You are so very old, of course."

"Thirty-two."

"Ah, of course. Ancient, in fact."

"To a college student."

"So there must be something really strange about

me… that I'm so very attracted to such an ancient specimen.''

Her words hit Steve like a sledgehammer in his solar plexus. "You're attracted to me?" he finally repeated.

"I thought kissing you at the pool was a strong indication, but you treated it so casually, I figured you weren't interested in me and you were just being gentle with my feelings. When you went to bed so early, I was even more convinced."

"You don't have any idea the struggle I've had keeping my hands off you, Ms. McAlister. If I'd known that you wanted—" He paused, searching for words.

"That I wanted to make love to you?" she asked.

"That wasn't what I was going to say!"

"But I do want to make love to you. I have for a long while, but I figured I wasn't your type. Of course, now that I know how ancient you are, I can better understand—"

His mouth effectively stopped her as he set about showing her just how very much she *was* his type, ancient though he might be.

He smoothed his hands over her body, tracing her spine, touching her breasts and thighs while he explored her mouth with increasing fervor.

She responded to him with such sweet eagerness that he was humbled.

He stroked her cheek and neck, resting his fingers on the rapid pulse at the base of her throat. She felt so fragile…delicate…and very precious to him.

When he paused to look at her, she smiled at him with all the allure of Eve. Her mouth was rosy, moist and slightly swollen, luring him to continue to taste and explore.

Steve caressed her neck and shoulder before cupping

her breast, which was barely covered by the bikini top she wore. Her breath caught, and he paused, his hand still.

"I can stop anytime you want, you know. All you have to do is tell me."

"I don't want you to stop," she whispered.

He closed his eyes, trying to gain some control over his reactions to her. He wanted this to be enjoyable for her.

He lowered his head and nuzzled her breast, edging the thin material to the side until her nipple was exposed. He toyed with the tip, using his tongue, until her nipple beaded up into a tight ball, then stroked it soothingly. He could feel her respond to each touch with first a quick gasp of air, then a slow sigh of pleasure.

He paused in his ministrations and kissed her mouth once again and discovered that she was a brilliant student—not only did she remember what they had done before but added a few variations of her own.

In fact, she was learning too fast, he discovered when her hands slipped from his shoulders to nimbly glide across his bare chest, pausing to tease his nipples until they hardened. When she leaned toward him and flicked her tongue across first one, then the other, he bit down hard on his bottom lip to keep from taking her right then.

With more haste than grace, he covered her breast and sat up, breathing heavily.

"What's wrong?" she asked. "Did I hurt you?"

He laughed. "Uh, not exactly. I'm trying to take this slow, but if you keep on like that, we'll be skipping a bunch of stages in this process."

She tilted her head and smiled at him, a smile full of seduction. "Then you liked me touching you?"

"Oh, yes," he said with a short nod. "Like doesn't

begin to describe it. I just don't want to rush you.'' He studied her for a moment before saying, ''Correct me if I'm wrong, but I got the impression that you aren't very experienced in these matters.''

''I'm sorry that I don't know much. If you could just show me—''

''Good grief, don't apologize for being innocent. I just want your first time to be a positive experience for you.''

He removed the wisps of her suit and allowed himself a moment to enjoy her beauty before quickly shucking his shorts and swimsuit.

He waited for her to take in his unclothed form. If he wasn't so aroused he would have been amused at her absorbed interest in him. Without a hint of shyness, she ran her fingers down his chest until she reached his male member. When he reacted to her touch, she smiled with pleasure.

She was too adorable for words and he couldn't wait any longer to have her. He leaned forward, his aroused flesh brushing against her. She sighed, bringing her knees up. He slipped his hand between them and was relieved to find she was ready for him. He reached into the pocket of his shorts and pulled out the foil package that he'd kept with him at all times since she'd shown up on the island.

Once protected, he knelt between her legs and slowly eased himself inside her until he felt the barrier that confirmed her lack of experience.

''Don't stop,'' she whispered, sounding desperate. ''Oh, please…don't stop.''

''I don't want to hurt you.''

She took matters into her own hands by suddenly lifting her hips in a strong surge, forcing him to go deep inside her. He gave up trying to move carefully and began a rhythm that would rapidly take him to completion. She'd made him forget everything but how good she felt and how much he wanted her.

He'd never felt like this with any woman before. It scared him to think how much he needed her. At that moment she began to whimper as she stiffened, holding him tightly to her. Her inner movements caused him to lose control, and he gave one final lunge before going over the edge and taking her with him.

By the time he could think once again, Steve lay beside her, holding her to him with no intention of ever letting her go. When she eventually stirred, he let out a sigh of remorse. "I'm sorry, love, but I lost it. I've never done that before and I—"

She placed her fingers over his lips. "You were magnificent. Please don't apologize."

He lay there a moment, dazed, before he grinned. "Magnificent? You think so? With all your vast experience, you think I'm the best, huh?"

"Without a doubt. I had no idea what I've been missing."

He laughed. She sounded so smug.

"Too bad you're leaving tomorrow."

She leaned on her elbow and looked at him, then trailed her fingers from his throat to his groin and back. "Well, we still have today, don't we?"

He chuckled. "I may not survive the day, but what a way to go."

Six

They were a little more than halfway back to the house when the rain started. Steve grabbed Robin's hand, and they sprinted along the beach until they reached the path leading up to the house. By the time they dashed inside, pulling the sliding glass door behind them, they were winded and soaked, rivulets of water making puddles on the floor.

Robin looked at Steve, still dazzled by the knowledge that she had actually made love with him—wonderfully fulfilling, intoxicating love. His curly hair was plastered around his head, and water was dripping down his face. She knew she must look just like him—a couple of drowned rats.

She laughed out loud and threw her arms around him.

He grabbed her and swung her up into his arms before striding down the hallway to the last door. She reached over and opened it for him, and he stepped inside. She got a vague sense of an oversize room that looked big enough for a basketball game before he walked into a bathroom that was close in size to the bedroom she'd been occupying. Obviously, whoever had designed this home wanted plenty of space.

The shower had double heads and was large enough for a party. Steve peeled off his clothes, then turned and removed her top and tugged at her bikini bottoms. When she stepped out of them, he moved over to the shower and turned both nozzles on, adjusting the water temperature before turning and beckoning her with a wicked smile on his handsome face.

She dreamed about that smile, so white in his darkly tanned face. She wasn't sure where her dreams left off and reality began. She couldn't get over the fact that all the time she was wishing that something would happen between them he'd been creating fantasies of his own.

Robin was more than happy to indulge him in those fantasies.

She stepped into the shower.

He took a loofah and rubbed soap on it until there was a lather, then he turned with a very wicked gleam in his eye and began to lightly rub it over her, starting at her shoulders, then down around and over her breasts, leaving a trail of bubbles that felt like silk against her skin.

She shivered at the sensuousness of the actions.

He turned her around and rubbed her back, causing her to arch like a cat in response. When he turned her to face him once more, she was so relaxed she could hardly stand.

He surprised her by kneeling in front of her before he once again rubbed the loofah over her, reaching around her to slide his hands across her buttocks. He leaned lightly toward her and kissed her nest of curls. Startled, she looked down at him in surprise.

"Steve, what are you— Oh, Steve, I—" Then she lost the power of speech as her mind went blank. She could only feel, and the sensations he was arousing in her were like nothing she had ever before experienced. He caressed her with his tongue and fingers, gently massaging her until her body seemed to explode with pleasure. He stood in time to grab her as her knees gave way.

"You okay?" he whispered, kissing her ear.

She could only nod.

He stepped back from her and began to rub the soapy loofah over his chest. She took it from him and carefully soaped his body, front and back, giving particular attention to that part of his body that seemed to have a mind of its own. By the time they rinsed off, he was fully aroused.

She'd had no idea that the male body could look so good in its unadorned, aroused state. She touched him, delighted to see an immediate response and to hear his groan of pleasure. He placed his hands on her waist and walked her backward into the bedroom until they reached the bed. He tossed the spread off the bed before placing her in the middle of it.

Robin lost track of time as her world narrowed to Steve and all that he taught her. There wasn't a part of her body that he didn't explore, stroke and caress. She quickly determined that he responded most enthusiastically when she explored him in the same way.

He made her feel sexy and seductive and encouraged her to touch him wherever and however she wished. They played until their passion could no longer be ignored, then made love, rested and dozed until one or the other started caressing and arousing the other once again.

At one time he teasingly told her that she had worn him completely out so that all he could do was just lie there and let her have her way with him. That's when he showed her how to sit astride him and control their coming together, laughingly pointing out that he had created a monster who was going to insist on being in control in the future.

He made her weak with love and with laughter. By the time she fell asleep in his arms she knew that this man had branded her with a fire she'd never forget.

When she awoke early the next morning, Robin wasn't certain where she was and if all that had happened had been a dream, until she turned her head on the pillow and saw Steve sprawled next to her on his stomach, his head beneath his pillow.

She smiled at the sight of his broad back, remembering the feel of it beneath her hands. She lay quietly, a sense of exhilaration sweeping over her. Yesterday had been so perfect, from the time she opened her eyes on the beach and saw him there until she fell into an exhausted sleep a few hours ago.

She couldn't imagine experiencing so much intimacy with anyone else. Steve had teased her about thinking he was a wonderful lover, but she knew the truth. She'd heard friends talk about sex, and more than one had considered it highly overrated. She'd been glad that she'd never been intimate with anyone before, that she had waited until the absolute perfect time.

She discovered that she was more than a little sore from all the unaccustomed activity and decided to slip out of bed and take a soothing soak in the tub.

Deciding not to disturb Steve, she returned to her bedroom. She went into the bathroom there and filled the tub with warm water and a herbal-salt mixture, then sank into the healing liquid with a sigh. She leaned her head back against the sloping back of the tub and closed her eyes. What a wonderful vacation this had been. There was so much that she wouldn't be able to share with Cindi, but, oh, she would never forget a single moment.

She was so glad that Steve had looked for her yesterday, grateful that he'd acknowledged his interest in her. She drifted into a state of steamy satisfaction, aroused when she heard Steve's voice calling.

"Robin? Robin, where are you! You had better be here, damn it! I don't want you leaving without—"

"Steve! I'm in here," she called, repeating herself in a louder voice until he pushed the door open and peered inside. "Good morning," she said, smiling at the look of rumpled grumpiness he wore. His hair stood out in a riot of curls around his face. He had on a pair of shorts and, as usual, no shirt or shoes.

He looked wonderful to her.

"You okay?" he asked, frowning down at her.

She wrinkled her nose at him. "Well, if you must know, I'm a little sore, but nothing that a nice soak in the tub won't help. We may have been a little over-enthusiastic yesterday."

He knelt by the tub and rubbed his knuckles against her cheek. "Oh, sweetheart. I'm so sorry. I never even thought— Of course you aren't used to—" He shook his head. "What was I thinking?"

"I don't think either one of us was doing much thinking."

He sat back on his heels. "I know. When I woke up and found you gone, I panicked. We're going to need to leave here in a couple of hours in order to get you to St.

Thomas in plenty of time to make connections with the ship. In the meantime—''

He paused, as though uncertain what to say.

Robin spoke. ''In the meantime...I need to gather my clothes, which as I recall are still in a sodden pile in your bathroom, and get them dry so I can be ready to leave.''

He touched her, running his hand along the tops of her breasts. ''I don't want you to leave,'' he said. ''I keep thinking of the first days you were here. Look at the time we wasted!''

''And all the money I won playing poker and pool. If I were to cash in those chips, I could afford to charter a plane back home,'' she teased.

''Do you realize I don't know how to reach you in Texas? I need a phone number, an address, something to—''

She sat up in the tub. ''Steve? Are you planning to stay in touch once we leave here?''

He frowned. ''Isn't that a given? There's no way we can just walk away from what we've discovered here.'' He slowly stood and looked down at her, ''Unless this was just some holiday fling you were having.''

''Of course not!'' She let the water out of the tub and stood, pulling a towel around her. Robin couldn't remember a time when she'd felt so vulnerable. She dried off and quickly put on the caftan Carmela had brought her.

He followed her into the bedroom and sat down on the vanity bench. ''Then what's the problem?''

She gave an embarrassed laugh, walking toward the window. ''Well, don't you see how awkward this is going to be? I don't intend for my family to find out about my stay here on the island. So I can't very well go back and tell them all about meeting you.''

She could feel his gaze boring into her back. When

she glanced over her shoulder, he said, "I never saw you as a coward, Robin."

She turned and faced him. "I never saw myself as a coward, either, but so much has happened and I'm not sure how to handle it."

"So rather than face up to what has happened, you want to hide it? Are you ashamed of what has happened?"

She looked away. "Not ashamed. Not exactly. Maybe I'm a little shocked at my behavior. But I'm not sorry that I met you, that we, uh, that I—"

He moved abruptly to the door. "I get the picture, Robin. Sorry I was so slow to understand. This is all you ever wanted—a vacation fling—and I happened to be conveniently available. Well, hey, that's fine with me. You certainly livened up my vacation for me." He turned away. "I'll go see when Romano will be ready to leave. We need to eat, as well."

Robin stared at the doorway where Steve had been. Boy, did she ever mess up that particular conversation. She hadn't said anything that she'd meant, nor explained how she felt about him.

Part of the reason was that she was truly confused about her feelings.

Weren't vacation romances almost a cliché? All the promises to see each other again, to write and stay in touch eventually lapsed as each of the parties returned to their regular life and routine.

Facing her family with the news of a romantic meeting while on vacation would be tough, but she would be willing to do that if there was a chance that she and Steve could have a lasting relationship.

He seemed really hurt by the idea that she might have

been using him. She had to make sure he understood that her feelings ran far deeper than that.

She went back to his bathroom and scooped up their wet clothes and the towels they'd used, then went to the other part of the house.

Steve was in the kitchen, sipping on coffee and eating one of Carmela's mouthwatering pastries.

"You misunderstood me," she said, then went into the washroom and put their clothes in the washer. When she came out, she poured herself a cup of coffee, grabbed one of the pastries off the tray and sat down across from him. "You are much more than a vacation fling to me."

He studied her in silence over the rim of his cup. Finally he said, "Glad to hear it."

"Here's the problem as I see it. We've been here alone for several days, and we've had a chance to get acquainted. But neither of us really knows what the other is like in our real life. We need that time, to see each other in our own environment, to decide—"

"Which is exactly what I was saying. We haven't taken the time to exchange addresses and phone numbers. I know that you're busy with school, but maybe on your spring break you could come to L.A. and let me show you around. We'll drive up to Santa Barbara and—"

She began to laugh. "Oh, Steve. If you could just understand how protective my family is! They threw a fit— at least my dad and brothers did—when I announced I was coming on this cruise. I would have three escorts if I attempted to visit you in L.A."

He leaned back in his chair. "Does that mean that they'd want to go on your honeymoon with you, as well?" he asked.

Robin could feel herself flushing. "Well, no, but since that isn't what we're talking about here—"

The Editor's "Thank You" Free Gifts Include:
- Two BRAND-NEW romance novels!
- An exciting mystery gift!

PLACE FREE GIFT SEAL HERE

YES! I have placed my Editor's "Thank You" seal in the space provided above. Please send me 2 free books and a fabulous mystery gift. I understand I am under no obligation to purchase any books, as explained on the back and on the opposite page.

326 SDL C6MD

225 SDL C6L7
(S-D-OS-11/00)

NAME (PLEASE PRINT CLEARLY)

ADDRESS

APT.# CITY

STATE/PROV. ZIP/POSTAL CODE

Thank You!

Offer limited to one per household and not valid to current Silhouette Desire® subscribers. All orders subject to approval.

The Silhouette Reader Service™ — Here's how it works:

Accepting your 2 free books and gift places you under no obligation to buy anything. You may keep the books and gift and return the shipping statement marked "cancel." If you do not cancel, about a month later we'll send you 6 additional novels and bill you just $3.34 each in the U.S., or $3.74 each in Canada, plus 25¢ shipping & handling per book and applicable taxes if any.* That's the complete price and — compared to cover prices of $3.99 each in the U.S. and $4.50 each in Canada — it's quite a bargain! You may cancel at any time, but if you choose to continue, every month we'll send you 6 more books, which you may either purchase at the discount price or return to us and cancel your subscription.

*Terms and prices subject to change without notice. Sales tax applicable in N.Y. Canadian residents will be charged applicable provincial taxes and GST.

"It could be," he said softly. "I don't want to lose you in my life, Robin. If it means getting married first and getting better acquainted afterwards I'd do it."

Robin fought down the panic his words caused her. "Married? You and me?"

He studied her in silence for several minutes, which didn't ease the tension between them in the slightest, then rolled his head on his neck in a silent acknowledgment of the tension. "Robin, I realize that you don't know me very well, but I'm not the kind of person to indulge in casual sex. I never have, and I certainly didn't decide to do so because I'm on vacation. I know we haven't known each other long enough to make long-term commitments, but we need to explore that option for later down the road. You're the first woman I've ever met to whom I'm ready to make a commitment, even if I met you less than a week ago. Are you saying you never considered marriage as an option?"

She dropped her head into both hands, her elbows resting on the table in front of her.

"I can see how thrilled you are at the prospect," he muttered, pouring another cup of coffee.

"It's not that."

"Oh?"

"At least, not exactly. What I mean is, we can't just rush into something on the basis of—"

"Of what? No matter how careful we were yesterday and last night, those things aren't 100 percent foolproof. And the truth is, I wouldn't care if you were pregnant. I'd like to have some time alone with you before we started a family, but—"

"You're serious, aren't you?" she whispered, her body shaking as though she were going into shock. And maybe she was. This was the last thing she thought might happen.

"Yes."

He let his stark answer hang in the air between them.

"I need more time," she finally said weakly.

"I'll give you all the time you need." He pushed back from the table and arose. "Let's check those clothes and see about getting you back to your ride home, okay?"

He went into the washroom, and she heard him moving the clothes to the dryer, and turning it on.

She lifted her cup with both hands and shakily sipped on her coffee.

He didn't say anything more. Neither did she. Her thoughts were whirling around like a cluster of tornadoes. Telling her family about meeting Steve was one thing. Telling them that he had proposed marriage was another.

They would think— Well, they would think exactly what had taken place. And there would be hell to pay. She didn't want to have to face the turbulent scenes, nor did she want them attacking Steve for something that she was responsible for creating. She had encouraged him every step of the way. She had wanted him to make love to her. She had wanted him to teach her all the pleasures that could be shared between a man and a woman.

He had done that. Oh, boy, had he done that.

Somehow, she had thought that she would be able to lock away all those experiences and go back to her life the way it had been before she met him. California had seemed like a safe place for him to live. If she'd given it any thought at all, she would have thought that they might exchange addresses and possibly Christmas cards. That he would be a wonderful memory she would always carry with her.

This was not turning out the way she had expected.

Not at all. And she had no one to blame but herself. In the few days she'd gotten to know Steve, she'd discovered that he was a man of integrity, a man who unabashedly loved his family. It was true that neither of them had discussed their attitudes toward matrimony, but Steve had talked about how tough his profession was on the men he worked with who were married. She had gotten the impression from their conversations that he preferred being single to trying to juggle a home life with his demanding profession.

Could she have made such an impression on him that he was willing to readjust his views? She was glad that he didn't consider her a casual encounter in his life. Of course she was. But she hadn't expected him to push for a serious relationship in such a short while.

Robin heard the door close behind her. Steve had left, probably to go see Romano. She needed to gather together the few things she'd brought with her.

When Steve returned she had everything in her bag and was pulling clothes out of the dryer.

"We'll be leaving as soon as you're ready," he said.

"Are you going with us?"

He said, "I know this may sound strange to you, but I'm not in a hurry to tell you goodbye. Do you have a problem with that?"

She smiled. "Not at all." She walked over to him and put her arms around his waist. "You are the best thing that ever happened to me, Steve. Just have a little patience with me, okay?"

He wrapped his arms around her and held her tightly. "You want to know the embarrassing truth? I'm scared to death of losing you. It seems as though I've waited for you my whole life. And I have this sinking feeling that once you leave this island you're going to disappear and I'll never see you again.''

She raised her head from his chest. ''That will never happen.''

''I'm going to trust that you mean that.'' He stepped away from her. ''And you'd better get some clothes on or I'm going to have you back in bed in two minutes flat.'' He ran his hands up her spine, then cupped her buttocks, pulling her hard against him, making sure she recognized just how aroused he was.

She stepped back from him, picked up the clothes from the dryer and hurried into the bedroom. When she came out, she discovered that he had also changed clothes.

He was dressed more formally than she'd ever seen him—in a pair of khaki pants and a Polo shirt with his dock shoes.

''I feel distinctly underdressed in my shorts and top.''

He took her hands and eased her closer until he could kiss her. ''Mmm. Thank you for that. And I like to see you underdressed.'' He reached into his pocket. ''Here's my card. I wrote my home address and telephone number on the back, so you can reach me at all times—either at work or at home. Just don't lose the card. My number's unlisted.''

She handed him a piece of paper. ''Here's my number and address.''

He carefully folded it and put it in his billfold. ''Thank you.'' He said it as though she'd given him an invaluable gift. ''We really need to go,'' he said, dropping his arm around her shoulders.

They went outside and down to where a dock jutted out into the water. Romano smiled and greeted them, before helping her board.

Steve followed.

They sat in the back while Romano sat in the captain's chair and steered them away from the dock, heading out to the open sea.

Steve wrapped his arm around her shoulders and Robin rested her head against his chest. The island quickly receded from view. She listened to the steady beat of his heart beneath her ear. It was hard to believe that her five days with him were over.

They'd spent so much of their time talking about their lives and yet had never discussed—until this morning—the connection they had made and what it might mean to their future.

Robin admitted that she was scared. She wasn't ready for this. She needed time away from Steve's magnetic personality to look more objectively at what had happened between them.

There was so much ahead of her that she'd looked forward to doing—taking the job with the agency, getting her own apartment, becoming independent of everyone. If she married Steve, she would become a part of another person's life and be expected to make compromises and deal with all kinds of issues she thought she wouldn't face for many years.

But the thought of never seeing him again scared her even more.

"Thank you for this week," she finally said.

He leaned down to hear her, then smiled at her words. "The pleasure was all mine. Believe me."

"How much longer will you be here?" she asked after a comfortable silence.

He shrugged. "I don't know. A week, maybe. I haven't decided. It isn't going to be the same without you."

The rest of the trip was filled with long silences and

casual remarks. Robin was surprised when she saw an island growing larger on the horizon. ''We're almost there,'' she said.

She had a sudden rush of relief as they drew closer and she saw the cruise ship sitting in the harbor. Steve directed Romano to take her directly to the ship. When they pulled alongside, one of the ship's crewmen was there to help her board.

She stood, trying to keep her balance in the rocking boat. ''Call me when you get back to L.A.,'' she said.

''You can count on it,'' Steve replied. He kissed her, a searing, devouring, possessive kiss that turned her knees to rubber and her brain to jelly.

When he finally let her go he stepped back and said, ''Take care of yourself for me, okay?''

She smiled, even though she felt tears welling up. ''You do the same.'' Then she clambered onto the ship and watched as the launch moved away. She waved at Steve and blew him a kiss, then turned and headed toward her room.

Her fantasy vacation was over. Would what they were feeling for each other last through the coming weeks and months?

She was afraid to guess. Either way, her life would never be the same again.

Seven

"**O**migosh! You're back! When did you get back? No-body told me that you were going to rejoin the cruise. I thought you'd already flown home! Oh, Robin, am I glad to see you!"

Robin groggily sat up in her bunk. She'd returned to their room and decided to take a nap. Now she stared in sleepy bewilderment at her exuberant roommate who had landed on the bed, talking a mile a minute.

"Was it horrible, being marooned on an island? I couldn't believe they actually went off and left you! How rude. I gave the captain my opinion of the crew's behav-ior, let me tell you. Of course, he reminded me of the rules and how often they had stressed them, but...still!" Cindi hugged her, then pulled away and stared at her. "Are you okay?"

Robin began to laugh. "Well, I thought I was, until Hurricane Cindi hit the room." She pushed her hair back from her face. "It's good to see you, too." Still chuckling, she added, "Did you really give the captain a bad time about leaving me behind?"

"Of course I did! You would have done the same for me. I was so worried that something awful had happened to you. At least they reassured me that you'd called to say you were all right. How in the world did you find a telephone?"

"Remember we were told that the island was privately owned?"

Cindi nodded.

"Well, there's this gorgeous home on the island with a caretaker couple who look after the place." She paused, carefully choosing her words. "There was a man who happened to be vacationing there who found me on the beach and invited me to return to the house with him. He was very kind. He contacted the cruise line and got the number of the ship for me so that I could call. Once he found out that the ship wouldn't be back in this area for another five days, he insisted that I share the house with him. He was really very nice to me."

Robin could almost see Cindi's ears perk up as she explained. "A *man?* You actually met a man while you were stuck on the island?" She broke into peals of laughter. "Leave it to you to have all the luck! So tell me about him!"

Robin shrugged. "I just did. He was very kind."

"So's my grandfather. You know what I mean! Is he young? Single? Good-looking?"

"Uh-huh."

"Uh-huh, what?"

"To all the above," she replied with a grin.

"What does he look like?"

She closed her eyes as though she had to recall what

had been engraved in her memory for the rest of her life. Then she shrugged in an attempt to sound casual. "Oh, you know, the usual kind of guy you'd find staying alone on an isolated island—tall, dark, extremely handsome, with the body of a Greek god, the intelligence of an Einstein, a great sense of humor, a—"

"Yeah, right. So, the truth is he was over sixty, fat, bald and a real lech, right?"

Robin sighed. "No, he really is a gorgeous hunk that could have made a living gracing the pages of women's magazines, Cindi. When I first saw him, I thought I'd died and gone to Heaven. He was like the answer to every woman's fantasies come to life."

Cindi's eyes grew wider as she listened. "You're not kidding me?"

Robin crossed her heart with her finger, then silently held her hand up in the sign of an oath. "Hope to die."

"Wow," Cindi breathed reverently. "And here I've been feeling so terribly sorry for you for missing the cruise and you were living this wonderful fantasy! You've got to tell me everything that happened! I mean everything. What's his name?"

"Steve Antonelli."

Cindi drew her brows together. "Antonelli, Antonelli. Why does that name sound familiar to me? Maybe he *is* a model or a movie star or something. Did he tell you what he does? Where he's from?"

"He's from L.A. He works for the LAPD."

"A cop?" Cindi repeated. "Really?" She rolled her eyes. Then she snapped her fingers and said, "I know! There used to be a Tony Antonelli who played baseball years ago. My dad thought he was the greatest player since DiMaggio. "

"Steve's dad. I'm embarrassed to admit I'd never heard of his father."

"Well, you've never been that interested in sports. So, I wasn't too far off, actually. He's a celebrity, once removed. What's he like? What did you guys do?"

She shrugged. "About what you'd expect, I guess. We swam in the ocean—oh, Cindi, you should have seen the beach. There was a lagoon that was sheltered from the big waves. It was like a giant swimming pool, really. The woman looking after the place was a great cook. She kept us fed. We explored the island, watched the sunset—you know, the usual things."

"Don't stop now!" her friend said with a hint of irritation. "What about at night? Did he come on to you? Well, of course he would. So then what?"

"Cindi, I swear you have a one-track mind at times."

"All right, so what did you do for entertainment?"

"The place was furnished like a private club. There was a pool table, table tennis and all kinds of games. We probably played our fair share of them."

"Was he surprised at how well you play pool, or did you decide to let him win, to save his ego."

"Nope. Beat his pants off."

"Literally?"

Robin rolled her eyes. "No. Not literally. He was a perfect gentleman the whole time I was there."

Cindi took her hand and stroked it with sympathy and sisterly commiseration. "Oh, Robin, honey. I'm so sorry to hear that. Do you suppose he's gay?"

"No! Of course he isn't gay. I mean, he showed some interest. He kissed me a few times. He gave me his card and said he wanted to keep in touch."

"Humph." Cindi got off the bed from her cross-legged position. "Five days with a sexy Italian stallion and all you can say about him is that he was kind and a gentle-man. Doesn't sound like much fun to me. So what were you doing asleep just now? It's almost time for dinner.''

Robin stretched and got out of bed. ''Just resting. I've been on the go since I last saw you. So, tell me every-thing I've missed in the past five days!''

''I've got so much to tell you, I'm not sure where to begin,'' Cindi replied. ''Let's get dressed and go to din-ner. There's a great floor show planned for later tonight. We've got to make the most of the rest of the cruise. We'll be back in Miami day after tomorrow.''

Later that night they made their way to one of the deck bars, ordered tropical drinks that were decorated with hanging fruit and umbrellas, and then they stretched out on the lounge chairs. The night breeze was a perfect com-plement to the evening. Robin gazed up at the stars and wondered what Steve was doing right at this moment. Was he looking at the stars? Thinking of her? Missing her?

She missed him, but she also realized how easy it had been to slip back into the camaraderie of being with her best friend. The island seemed to be receding into some magical place in her mind—where she'd met and made love to the perfect man, the perfect lover. Anything more that happened between them would be anticlimactic. Wouldn't it?

If so, why did she miss him so much? Why did she want to tell him about the evening's entertainment, share some of the jokes told by the headlining comic?

She needed to talk to someone about all her confusing feelings and yet, when Cindi offered—insisted, actu-ally—on knowing what had happened, she couldn't tell her. She couldn't reduce all the many emotions she'd experienced to words. There were no words to describe what being with Steve meant to her.

"You asleep?" Cindi finally asked, and Robin realized how long she'd been silent.

"No, of course not. You told me all the things you did, the places you saw, but what about—" she paused dramatically "—a man. Surely you met someone during those day trips?"

Cindi laughed. "Actually, I did."

"Really! And you never mentioned it. I like that, after you were so insistent on hearing about my time away."

"Well, I really think he started talking to me because we were both alone, so I felt a little guilty about mentioning it to you. I mean, I didn't want you to think that with you gone I was able to run wild in the streets."

"I wouldn't think that. So. Tell me."

Cindi smiled reminiscently. "His name is John Taylor. He goes to Yale—prelaw. We really hit it off. He and his roommate had made plans to spend the week in St. Croix until his roommate backed out at the last minute and he decided to come down by himself. I explained what happened to you, and we laughed about fate throwing us together. We spent most of the day together." She looked at Robin. "I really liked him, Robin. And he seemed to think I was pretty special, too. It's hard to explain, how you can meet someone and not be with them very long and yet feel as if you've known them forever."

"I know."

Cindi shrugged. "We exchanged phone numbers and addresses, but I'm not going to hold my breath to see if I hear from him. He made the day really fun, but I don't want to start building pipe dreams about what may happen next.''

''Neither do I.''

Robin woke early the next morning suffering with abdominal cramps and the certain knowledge that there was no chance of her being pregnant. Of course she was relieved. The last thing she needed to face right now was an unexpected pregnancy.

She remembered what Steve had said about wanting to have children with her. She needed to call and let him know that there would be no repercussions from their time on the island. At least, none that were visible.

She felt so different from the woman who had gone to visit the tide pools last week—the one whose biggest concern in life was her brothers' overprotectiveness. Now she was looking at being involved with a man who worked in a very dangerous profession, who lived a thousand miles away and who made her tremble at his touch. She was afraid of what she felt. Afraid of losing who she was before she ever had a chance to truly find out for herself.

After taking some pain medication for her cramps, Robin crawled back into bed. When Cindi stirred, she told her about her physical condition and that she thought she'd stay in bed for the day. They'd be back in Miami tomorrow, then would catch their return flight back to Texas.

Once she was home, Robin would decide what she needed to do.

Robin had been home for three days. It was the first evening that Cindi had gone out, so Robin was alone. She pulled out Steve's card from her purse, carefully studying it. Then she placed it on the table, picked up the phone and called his home number.

Voice mail immediately came on in Steve's voice, saying, "Please leave a message."

She hadn't really expected him to answer, although he had made it sound as though there was some question about his staying on alone; that once she was gone his vacation would no longer be as much fun for him. Obviously, he'd chosen to stay on the island.

She swallowed, then began her message.

"Hi, Steve. This is Robin. Just called to let you know that everything is fine with me. No long-lasting effects from being on the island. My life is back to normal. The new semester started yesterday. I'm going to be really busy this spring. I want to thank you once again for your hospitality. I enjoyed getting to know you. Thanks for making my vacation so memorable."

There. That had been casual enough, she hoped. She didn't want to sound like she was sitting beside her phone waiting for him to call....

A week went by.

Then another.

And another...

She never heard from him.

As time passed, it slowly became obvious to Robin that everything Steve Antonelli had said to her was a lie.

She'd stayed home yet another night with the excuse that she needed to study when it dawned on her how stupid she was being, to think he was actually going to get in touch with her.

He had accused *her* of using him for a vacation fling.

What a laugh.

No wonder the accusation had come so glibly to his tongue. It was what he'd had in mind all along. And to think that she had actually believed he was serious when he'd brought up the subject of marriage!

He had completely convinced her of his sincerity. How naive could she be? He must be laughing his stupid head off with his buddies back in L.A at her gullibility.

She *should* have made him pay for all those games of pool and poker he'd lost to her! She picked up the card he'd given to her, had *insisted* on giving her, and shook her head in disgust.

No more moping around, she decided. She tossed the card in the wastebasket and walked out. She'd go to a movie, look for some friends, go shoot some pool. She would do something besides sit at home waiting for the phone to ring.

As far as she was concerned, Steve Antonelli was history.

Eight

———

Los Angeles, California
Late March

And now we return to Steve's unexpected
encounter with Robin's irate brothers...

Steve studied the three men lined up before him, looking
for some resemblance to Robin. Once he got past their
obvious toughness, he saw a glint of green in one pair of
eyes, a reddish hue in the hair of another. These must be
the brothers she'd told him about—the ones who'd honed
her skills to play poker and shoot pool.

He was having a little trouble visualizing her spending
much time with these characters, but then, hadn't he
eventually realized that he hadn't really known Robin at
all?

"Did Robin send you here?" he finally asked out of curiosity.

For several moments no one spoke. Then the oldest reached into his pocket and pulled out a card. He handed it to Steve. "You gave this to her, didn't you?"

He took the card and flipped it over, looking down at his handwritten note. "That doesn't answer my question. Does Robin know you're here?"

The men shifted their booted feet, but no one spoke.

Steve crossed his arms. "I'm beginning to get the picture here. Robin told me about you guys—how you love to meddle in her life, follow her everywhere she goes like a pack of wolves, intimidate anyone who shows any interest in her. So now you've decided to take up the slack. Since you weren't with her on her vacation, you figure anyone she saw would automatically take advantage of her."

The one referred to as Jim said, "You telling us you didn't take advantage of her?"

Steve kept his gaze level. "That's exactly what I'm telling you. Not that it's any of your business, but the reason I gave her this card was not so you could hunt me down and cart me back to Texas to make an honest woman of your sister. Actually, I had hoped that she would want to stay in touch, maybe give us a chance to get to know each other better. However, she made it clear that she wasn't interested in pursuing a relationship of any kind with me."

"Oh? How did she do that?" their leader asked.

Steve knew his smile was cold. "She conveniently gave me a wrong number to call when we exchanged information. I got some guy on the phone who'd never heard of her. When I couldn't get a telephone listing for her, I finally figured out that she hadn't wanted to tell me to my face that she didn't want to hear from me."

"Cindi said something about Robin not wanting to talk about him, remember?" one of them muttered below his breath.

"Cindi? Her roommate?" Steve asked.

"Do you know her?" the leader said.

"No, but I know about her. She and Robin have been friends since grade school."

The leader stepped forward and said, "Look, maybe we went about this the wrong way. Would you mind if we start all over?" Before Steve could suggest they start all over by getting the hell out of his house, the man went on. "My name is Jason McAlister, Jr. These are my brothers, Jim and Josh. I'm afraid that Robin may have given you the wrong impression about us."

"Oh, I don't think so. Breaking and entering is illegal. The fact that you did it to a Los Angeles police officer is the height of arrogance, just to begin with. I have no trouble believing that the three of you have made her life a living hell. In fact, after meeting you I can well understand why she wants nothing to do with any man."

"Now, just wait a minute," Josh said, bristling with indignation. "I'm not going to take anything off you, I don't care what police force you happen to work for!"

Steve looked at Jason. "Your brother's hotheaded temper is going to get him in trouble one of these days."

Jason's nod was almost imperceptible. He glanced at Josh. "Cool it, bro. We all know how tough you are."

Steve almost smiled at the flush of color that washed over Josh's cheeks. He probably looked more like Robin than any of them.

Steve unfolded his arms and said, "Look, we obviously need to talk. I don't know about you, but I could use some coffee. Let's go downstairs and I'll make us some.'' While he talked he walked to the door as though the other two weren't still blocking it. Josh showed a continued reluctance to move, but Jim gave him a flashing grin—another reminder of Robin, that dimpled grin—and stepped out of his way.

It was Jim who said, ''Sounds good. It's been a while since our last stop for refreshments of any kind.''

Once downstairs, Steve motioned them to sit down. ''How did you get here, anyway?''

Jim answered. ''Jase flew us out in his plane. We rented a car at the airport. We figured the less anyone knew about our being here, the better.''

''You are aware that I could arrest all three of you, don't you? I've got enough to put you behind bars for a healthy length of time.''

Jim laughed. ''Ah, you don't want to do that. That's no way to start married life—locking your brothers-in-law away in some musty ol' jail.''

Steve shut his eyes and silently counted to himself. ''Look, guys, I don't know how you got that idea that I'm going to marry Robin, but you are so very wrong.'' He thought back to that polite little message that had been waiting for him when he got home. It had been a definite kiss-off. He just hadn't recognized it as such at the time. ''I'm curious as to why you think I should.''

Jason and Jim looked at Josh. ''Go on...tell him,'' Jason said.

Steve bit his lip to keep from grinning at the look of horror on Josh's face. ''I can't talk about it. I told you. I promised Cindi not to say a word.''

''You broke that promise when you told us. Now tell him.''

Josh sighed, looking at his brothers with a great deal

of disgust. "Oh, all right, but Cindi's going to kill me," he said dejectedly.

"I have a hunch she'll have to take her place in line, right after Robin," Steve replied. "Depending on your story, I might be right there with them, as well." He poured them all some coffee, dug around in his refrigerator and found some rolls and stuck them in the toaster oven to warm before setting them on the table. He sat down and waited.

Josh scratched his ear, then said, "Well, I happened to see Cindi the other day at school and asked her where Robin was. That's when she told me how worried she was about Robin."

Steve straightened in his chair. Was something going on that he didn't know about? Her message had made a veiled reference that she wasn't pregnant. Had she lied about that as well?

"Did she say why?" he asked, when Josh didn't appear to want to continue with his story.

Josh glared at him. "Yeah, as a matter of fact, she said that Robin hadn't been herself since they'd come back from their cruise. That's when she let it slip that Robin had gotten marooned on an island for half the trip, something that our dear sister had omitted to tell any of us when she got back. So I started asking all kinds of questions. That's when Cindi gave me that card. She said she found it in their wastebasket and she recognized your name. Robin had mentioned that you were on that island, as well, but she hadn't talked about you at all since she'd returned home. Cindi thinks something happened on that island that Robin doesn't want to talk about. Whatever it was has changed Robin. Cindi said she's aged—"

"Or maybe she just managed to grow up," Steve offered with a hint of sarcasm.

Jason leaned back in his chair. "That's my opinion, as well. And I was thinking about all the ways a young, very attractive, very innocent woman might suddenly grow up in a few days after spending time alone with a man Cindi kept referring to as the Italian stallion."

"What?" Steve almost dropped his cup full of hot coffee. "Where in the hell did you get that?"

Josh answered, sounding defensive. "Well, that's the way Cindi kept referring to you. I thought maybe it was your nickname or something. For all we know, you could be moonlighting as a stripper somewhere."

Steve laughed. It was either that or plant his fist in the kid's face. This whole thing was becoming more and more bizarre.

"Let me see if I get this straight. You are concerned about your sister because she's acting more mature these days? Is that right?"

Jason leaned his arms on the table and leaned toward Steve, his gaze direct and very cold. "We're here, hotshot, because I for one think that something happened to her on that island that had no business happening. That's what I think. It's the only explanation for her odd behavior. I don't believe in beating around the bush and I'm not asking you any direct questions that will cause you to make up a bunch of lies. Let's just say that I know human nature. The way I figure it, you put two attractive people on an island together for several days and one thing's going to lead to another. Add to that the fact that Cindi says that Robin hasn't heard anything from you since she got back—"

"Of course she hasn't! I've already told you, she made up a number that wasn't hers because she didn't intend to ever hear from me again!"

Jason continued as though Steve had never said a

word. "In this case your stay on that island is going to
lead to a wedding before the month is out."

"You can't force us into getting married," Steve said,
knowing he sounded belligerent. He no longer cared.
He'd had it up to here with the whole lot of them. If he
never saw another McAlister for the rest of his life, he
would die a happy man.

"You think not?" Jason asked, deliberately drawling
his words. "Well, you just hide and watch."

Nine

Steve strolled around the University of Texas campus, admiring the buildings, the statues, the Tower and the stadium. He was a little surprised at how warm it was for this time of year. He'd been wandering the grounds looking at everything for the past forty minutes and had become increasingly aware of the balmy air.

He glanced at his watch. According to Josh, Robin should be getting out of her last class of the day in about ten minutes. He planned to time his arrival at that particular building when she would be coming out.

One thing Steve could say about Texans, they certainly were determined to get their own way. The fact that he was here in Texas was actually the result of a compromise he'd made with Robin's brothers.

They agreed that they wouldn't insist that he marry her if he'd return to Texas with them and meet with her, find out why she'd lied to him, and, if possible, find out what it was about her changed behavior that had caused Cindi to worry about her. If she made it clear that she wanted no part of him, then they'd let him off the hook.

A generous offer in their minds.

It didn't matter to them that he had no more time coming and that his paycheck would reflect the loss of wages because of this trip. Once Steve discovered that Robin's best friend—as well as her brothers—was worried about her, he knew he wouldn't be able to forget about this whole mess until he found out what was going on by facing her for one final—and no doubt humiliating—time.

The fact that he actually wanted to see her again was the humiliating part—enough to lie to his captain and tell him he had a family emergency. He could lose his job over this little escapade.

As the time drew close for her to appear, Steve grew increasingly nervous. What if he didn't recognize her? Since coming on campus, he'd spotted several tall, slender women striding about the place. And they all seemed to dress the same—in battered jeans and oversize shirts or sweaters, their hair hidden by a variety of hats and caps.

The embarrassing truth was, he wasn't at all sure he'd recognize Robin with clothes on, something he definitely hadn't wanted to mention to her brothers.

Later, he realized he shouldn't have worried. He spotted her immediately by the way she walked, the tilt of her head, the way she wore her jeans, not to mention that glorious head of red hair flowing around her face and shoulders. Oh, yes. He would have known her anywhere.

He'd worn dress slacks and a sports jacket for this meeting, but had drawn the line at a tie. He wore his long-sleeved shirt with the collar open and was considering draping his jacket over his shoulder. Seeing her had already increased his body's temperature.

She didn't see him, but then there was no reason for her to be looking for him. Her brothers had suggested that he might prefer to surprise her. Actually, they had decided that the less she knew about their involvement in his sudden appearance, the better chance there was of keeping harmony in the family.

Since he knew quite well what she was going to do when she heard about their visit to California—and he had every intention of informing her—he could understand their concern about her reaction. It would almost be worth hanging around to watch her strip their hides off them.

He couldn't feel sorry for them. They needed to learn to butt out of other people's business, even if the people were loved ones. He'd learned that the hard way watching his brothers and sisters grow up.

It was time for her brothers to be taught a thing or two. Too bad he wasn't going to stick around long enough to do the teaching himself, but he had a strong hunch that Robin could take them on just fine.

He waited until she was even with him before he spoke her name. She jumped as though something had touched her with an electric prod and spun around in a circle with a haunted look in her eyes. Now that she was closer, he could see why her friend and family might be worrying about her.

She'd lost weight, and from the shadows beneath her eyes, it looked to him as if she'd lost more than a few nights' sleep, as well.

When she focused on him, her eyes widened and she turned pale beneath her tan. He stepped forward and took her arm, afraid she might faint. She jerked her arm away from him.

"What are you doing here!" she snapped, looking around as though afraid to be seen talking with him.

Her attitude confirmed what he'd already known—that he was the last person she wanted to see. But he was here now and, by damn, he was going to deal with the situation. Nobody would ever accuse *him* of being a coward.

"I was wondering if there's someplace we could go for a drink and maybe talk."

He wouldn't have thought she could look any paler, but she whitened even more with his words.

"I don't understand why you're here," she said stubbornly.

"Yes, I know that, which is why I'm suggesting we find a more private place where I can explain." He looked around at the stream of students walking around them.

She followed his gaze, finally taking notice of the people around them. "I suppose," she said, showing little enthusiasm.

One thing for sure. The meeting thus far couldn't be considered a roaring success.

It hadn't occurred to him that she would be *this* upset at seeing him again. Annoyed, perhaps. After all, she'd sent him a clear message, both on the machine and by giving him the wrong number, that she'd already dismissed him from her life.

Which was fine with him. Hell, he'd been busy getting on with his life, hadn't he? If it hadn't been for those blasted brothers of hers.

Once again he took her arm and started toward the parking lot. "Where are we going?" Her voice echoed her unease.

"I'm not kidnapping you, if that's what's bothering you. I'm going to the car. I thought we'd get away from the campus, if that's all right with you. What's the matter with you, anyway? You're acting like I'm some kind of stalker. I think that it's important that we talk. Otherwise, I wouldn't be here."

She glanced at him, then away, as though even the sight of him disturbed her. He didn't like this at all. Something was going on with her, and he'd find out before he left Texas or know the reason why.

She turned and started toward the parking lot, her book bag hanging off one shoulder.

When they reached his rental car, he opened the door for her, then walked around and got in on the other side. "Okay," he said. "Where to?"

She directed him off campus and several blocks farther, to a restaurant that had some tables out beneath large trees. They parked and found a table, gave drink orders to the waiter, then sat quietly, warily eyeing each other.

"You don't look like you've been getting much sleep," he finally said.

She shrugged. "I've been doing a lot of studying." Her lashes flickered, her gaze quickly going over him before she looked away. "You look as though your vacation agreed with you."

"It did. Particularly the part that was shared with you."

"Please don't go there, okay? I don't want to talk about that."

He studied her for a long while before leaning back in his chair with a distinctly sinking feeling. What in the world had he done to her that she could barely look at him, didn't want to talk with him? Had being with him in some way driven her over the edge so that now she disliked all men?

Or was it just him?

"I'm sorry," he finally said.

Their drinks arrived, along with a basket of tortilla chips and a bowl of red salsa.

She'd just reached for a chip when he spoke. She glanced up at him. "For what?" she asked warily.

"For whatever I did to make you dislike me so."

Her eyes widened and she began to laugh, but Steve didn't hear much amusement in the sound. "Well, let me count the ways...for making me feel like a naive fool, perhaps? For making that big scene the morning I left about how special I was, after all that had happened between us, talking about *marriage*, of all things, when it was all fun and games with you. You never meant a word of all that. And you accuse *me* of being a coward? At least I was honest with you when I told you I was confused about everything that had happened so quickly. I wanted to take it easy, to let things develop between us naturally...and you made me feel that *I* was using *you!*"

He shook his head. "You're a real piece of work, Robin. Just how—if you don't mind explaining this to me—did you see our relationship developing naturally when you deliberately gave me a fictitious number to call? Oh, not to mention that brush-off message you left on my voice mail to greet me when I got back home."

"I don't have the foggiest idea what you're talking about. I gave you my number, yes. It wasn't a fictitious number, by the way. And my message had nothing to do with a brush-off. It was a carefully worded message that I was not pregnant and that you didn't have to worry." As she talked her face became more flushed as her voice became quieter and more intense.

Steve was used to dealing with all kinds of people in all kinds of situations. He was good at reading people. It was obvious to him that Robin passionately believed what she was saying.

He considered what she'd said. So maybe her message hadn't been quite the brush-off he'd decided it was. It had sounded polite enough when he'd heard it the first time. In fact, he well remembered how delighted he was that she had called him.

He pulled out his billfold and pulled out the evidence he had that she had misled him. Like a good cop, he hadn't destroyed the evidence, even though he'd had absolutely no use for it once he discovered the truth.

Without saying a word, he handed the slip of paper to her, then crossed his arms and waited.

She glanced at it, then at him. "Is this supposed to be making a point? Because if it is, I've missed it."

"That's the number you gave me, and it belongs to some guy named Greg Hanson."

"That's bull. You dialed the wrong number."

"I might have. Once. Possibly twice. But I called that number so many times that Greg and I got on a first-name basis pretty quickly."

She looked at the paper again. "You dialed 555-2813?" she asked.

"You mean 2873."

"No. My number is 2813, which is what I wrote down. Right there." She poked her finger at the paper with a stabbing motion.

"That's not a one. It's a seven."

"Excuse me, but I believe I know my own telephone number."

"Well, I dialed a seven."

"Good for you."

They stared at each other in frustration and anger.

Steve looked at the piece of paper. He picked it up and stared at it closer. "That sure looks like a seven to me."

"So you keep saying."

He finished his drink and signaled the waiter for another one. He was beginning to feel much better about things. Much, much better. He might even have reason to be grateful to Robin's nosy, interfering brothers.

Cautiously Steve said, "So you really gave me the correct phone number." He said quietly, "You intended for me to call you."

She stared at him with disgust. "You actually thought that I would— You believed that after the time we had together that I'd—" Then something shifted, a light in her eyes or something about her expression, as though she'd just realized something. She tilted her head and aimed that heart-melting smile of hers directly at him. "You've been trying to call me," she said, wonder in her voice.

"Haven't I just made it abundantly clear that I spent an inordinate amount of time calling you? And getting friendly with good ol' Greg?"

She dipped her head and played with her glass. "I thought you blew me off after I left the island."

"What?"

She lifted her shoulders in a small shrug. "Well, when I didn't hear from you, I thought…" She let her words dwindle into silence.

"That everything I'd said to you on the island was a lie," he finally finished for her.

She nodded.

"Well, thanks for all that trust you have in me."

"You're saying *you* trusted *me?* Accusing me of giving you the wrong number as though I hoped to avoid you?"

They glared at each other.

"Would you like to hear the chef's suggestions for the evening, or would you prefer to look at our dinner menu?" the waiter asked.

Steve glanced up blankly, then focused on his surroundings. It had grown dark since they had arrived. Now several lamps and a myriad of tiny lights strung through the trees lit the area. Many of the tables around them were filled.

"Uh, give us a minute, if you please," he finally said.

The waiter nodded and walked away.

He looked at Robin. "I don't know about you, but I'm starved. Do you want to stay and eat?"

She, too, had only now noticed that the restaurant was getting busy. Her mouth twitched as though she were fighting a smile. "If you'd like," she said with dignity, then ruined the effect by chuckling. "I can't believe we're arguing about who is the abused party here, can you?"

"Well, you've got to admit this was quite a mix-up."

She reached over and took his hand. "Thank you for swallowing your pride and coming to see me," she said, softly. "I've missed you so much, but was determined not to chase you. I felt that I had made the first move by leaving you a message."

He grinned, taking her hand and bringing it to his mouth, where he pressed a kiss in her palm. "Too bad you didn't repeat your phone number. Then I would have heard it."

"Do you really think my ones look like sevens?"

He laughed. "I'm going to forgive you, okay? Now we'd better order before we get thrown out of here."

Once they were through with dinner, they returned to the car. As soon as Steve closed his door he reached for her. She flowed into his arms with reassuring eagerness.

The kiss was filled with pent-up passion that had them both aroused and trembling. When he finally pulled away from her, Steve placed his hand against her cheek. "Come back to the hotel with me. Will you?"

"I want to, Steve, but I can't. I need to get back to the apartment. Cindi's probably got the police out looking for me already. She's gotten to be such a mother hen, lately."

"Call her. Tell her you're fine. And that you'll see her in the morning."

She blinked, then slowly smiled. "All right."

Her agreement surprised him. It also told him that she was indeed maturing, making decisions for herself.

He'd rented a room at one of the hotels on the way to the new airport. Once at the hotel, he took her to his room. After unlocking the door, he motioned to the phone.

She quickly dialed a number and waited.

"Hi, Cindi, it's me," she said after a moment. "I'm fine. Yeah, I knew you'd be starting to worry, which is why I'm calling. Look, I ran into a friend, so I won't be home for a while. I just wanted to let you know I'm all right. I'll talk to you tomorrow."

She hung up, then turned around and looked at him. "You said we needed to talk."

He nodded. "I think we've done that."

"Yes, I guess we have. We seemed to have discovered that we have a few trust issues where the other is concerned."

"I think I have a solution for that."

"What's that?"

"Let's get married," he said lightly. "With that kind of commitment between us, I know we'll work out any minor kinks that might show up from time to time."

"You want to marry me because…?"

He walked over to her. "Because I love you," he admitted quietly. "I must have fallen in love that first day you appeared on the island. I know I've never been able to get you out of my mind since then. You're with me whether I'm asleep or awake, daylight or dark, on the job or at home. It ripped me apart to think that you didn't feel the same way."

"I would never have made love to you if I hadn't known how very much I love you."

He sighed in relief. "I was counting on that. That was the only thing that gave me any confidence to approach you there on the island. I knew that your innocence wasn't just a result of having protective brothers. You had chosen not to become intimate with anyone for a specific reason. The fact that you changed your mind where I was concerned was the most encouraging thing that happened."

"Please don't bring up my brothers, okay? When I got home I finally faced them and told each of them what I thought of their behavior and that I had had enough of it. I let them know in no uncertain terms that if they wanted any relationship with me, now or in the future, they were to stay out of my life."

Steve tried not to wince. Obviously her lecture hadn't fazed them in the least when they decided to come hunt him down.

Not that he blamed them. He would be eternally grateful that they had come looking for him.

"So, does this mean you'll marry me?"

She laughed and threw herself into his arms. "You bet.

I'm going to insist you make an honest woman of me. But we can talk about all the details later.'' She kissed him, then kissed him again with much more intensity. ''I don't know how long you can stay—''

''I need to go back tomorrow. My supervisors frown on my using up all my vacation time and then asking for more time off.''

''There's no need to rush, is there? I want us to take time to plan. Because Mom and Dad ran off and got married, she's always wanted me to have a large church wedding with all the trimmings. Those take time to arrange.''

''Plus the logistics of getting all my family from California to Texas for the ceremony. You're right,'' he said, scooping her up, ''the details can work themselves out. In the meantime…''

He decided to show her instead of tell her what he had in mind. Steve placed her on the bed and carefully unbuttoned her shirt, then unfastened her jeans, sliding them down her long, shapely legs.

He wanted to take his time and enjoy every inch of her. However, he wasn't sure he had that kind of restraint.

''I didn't expect to ever make love to you again,'' he admitted, placing tiny kisses along her neck and shoulders, then down to the top of her bra. He unfastened it, tossing it aside. He stroked the tip of her breast with his tongue, smiling when she squirmed beneath him.

''You're still dressed,'' she complained, pushing at his shirt. ''I can't get used to seeing you in clothes. I keep thinking of your bare chest when I visualize you.''

He sat up and quickly removed his clothing before stretching out on the bed beside her once more. She immediately ran her fingers over his chest, causing his skin to ripple in response.

As though impatient, Robin suddenly pushed him over on his back and straddled him. She leaned forward and rubbed her breasts against him, then started kissing him, seductively using her tongue to tease and provoke him. With a strangled laugh, he relaxed and said, "Take me. I'm yours."

"You'd better be," she whispered, arousing him to a fever pitch before finally sheathing him and riding him to a tumultuous climax that left them both quivering and breathlessly holding each other.

They dozed. Steve awoke sometime later when he heard a noise in the room. He opened his eyes and discovered that Robin had gotten out of bed. She stood at the window looking out, wearing his shirt.

It looked sexy as hell on her. She'd rolled the sleeves to her elbows. The tail hit her high on her thighs. She appeared pensive.

"What's wrong?" he asked, propping himself up on a couple of the pillows.

She turned and looked at him. They'd left the lamp on the dresser lit, but the rest of the room was in shadows. He couldn't see her expression but he could sense her mood.

"I just don't want us to rush into something we're going to regret, that's all," she said quietly. "This happened so fast. It's really scary. I look back at my folks. My mom had known Dad all her life. He lived on the adjoining ranch. She said she couldn't remember a time when she didn't love him. She never doubted those feelings."

"You're doubting what you feel?"

"Not now. No. I just wonder if these feelings will last. We've only known each other a couple of months."

"I know. As a matter of fact, my folks grew up next

door to each other, as well. But that didn't happen to you and me. We'll have to deal with it.''

She walked over and sat down at the foot of the bed. ''Other than summer jobs, I've never worked. There's so much I've not done that I want to do.''

''Are you afraid I'll stop you from doing them?''

''Maybe. I guess I'm more afraid that I'll become so wrapped up in you that I'll no longer care about growing as a person.''

He sat up and reached for her hand. ''Honey, being married to me will be a real stretch from what you've known in life. It will force you to grow, ready or not. I'm not trying to make you into something you aren't or don't want to be. All I'm asking is that we face life together, make our decisions together, work out the problems that come up in the same way.''

''We'll live in L.A., won't we?''

''I'm afraid so. That's where I work.''

''Would you ever consider getting similar work in Texas, in some law enforcement field here?''

He thought about that. Finally he said, ''I'm not averse to it, no. I've always lived in California, but if you don't think you'll be happy there, I'll rethink my position.''

''We could try it. I just don't know how I'll feel being so far away from my family.''

He grinned. ''You mean to tell me you're going to miss those brothers of yours?''

She laughed. ''Probably. I know they'll give me hell for marrying someone not from Texas.''

''Let's don't start worrying about things that might never happen, okay?'' He tugged on her hand until she tumbled down on the bed beside him. ''Whatever happens, we're going to make this work. You have my promise on that.''

He held her close, wondering exactly how to tell her that her brothers were going to be delighted that she was going to marry him.

Ten

The next morning Steve drove Robin back to her apartment. He parked in front of the building a little after eight o'clock. She had a ten-o'clock class.

Robin wanted to pinch herself to be sure she wasn't dreaming. Steve was actually here in Austin. He'd come to find her. He hadn't been feeding her a line when they met. He had made it very clear that he sincerely wanted to marry her.

Yes, she was scared, but not of loving him. She just wasn't ready to have such a man walk into her life at this time, but she wasn't about to let him go now that he was there.

As he'd said, they could work it out.

He opened her door and she stepped out. The sun shone brightly and all was right with her world. "I've got to get back to L.A. today, sweetheart, but as soon as you can find a few days, I want you to fly out and meet my parents. They're going to love you.''

''I was hoping you could stay long enough for us to drive to Cielo. I've got to break the news to my parents that I've not only met and fallen in love with someone, but intend to marry him as soon as we can arrange it.''

''We've got time to do all of that.'' He kissed her again.

''Well, hello-o-o-o there,'' Cindi said from somewhere behind her. ''When you said you'd see me this morning, that was exactly what you meant! I just about dropped my teeth when I got up this morning and discovered you hadn't come home last night.''

Robin spun around at the sound of her roommate's voice. ''Oh, hi, Cindi,'' she said a little weakly. She knew she looked guilty as she said, ''I—uh, thought you had an early class.''

Cindi grinned. ''I just bet you did.'' She looked Steve over very carefully, making it quite clear that she was quite impressed with what she saw. ''And just where have you been hiding, sugar? I can't believe that Robin's been seeing someone who I never knew existed.''

''Steve, as you've no doubt figured out, this mouthy female is my roommate, Cindi Brenham.'' She gave her friend a look of warning that she'd better behave herself or face the consequences before she added, ''Cindi, this is Steve Antonelli.''

Cindi grabbed Steve's hand with unfeigned enthusiasm and said, ''I am so very pleased to meet you, Steve. Obviously Robin was afraid to let me get a peek at you before now for fear that I would—'' Cindi came to a sudden halt, staring at Steve as his name finally registered. ''Wait a minute. Did you say Steve Antonelli? The cop from L.A.? The Italian stallion? Wow! No wonder she flipped out over you. This is *so* fantastic." She pumped his hand vigorously. "It's great to finally meet you. I wish I could say I've heard all about you, but my dear roommate can at times make a clam appear chatty. She never mentioned what a dreamy hunk you are, the rat!"

Robin was used to Cindi but she could see that Steve was more than a little startled by her comments. His cheeks turned ruddy, and he appeared to be at a loss for words.

But not Cindi. If Robin had been standing closer, she would have kicked her! She continued to chatter. "I can't believe you're here after all this time. So Jason managed to hunt you down, didn't he? I figured he might. He's quite resourceful when he's on a mission. It looks as though everything has worked out just fine." She turned to Robin. "So—when's the wedding?"

Robin was fighting to come to grips with what she'd just heard. She looked at Cindi, then at Steve—a Steve who had a distinctively sheepish look on his face.

"Jason?" she repeated.

"Uh, Robin, I," Steve began, then stopped.

Cindi looked at Steve. "Well, that *is* the reason you showed up here, isn't it? Didn't Cindi's brothers go after you and insist you come back and do the right thing by their sister?"

Steve avoided Robin's gaze by concentrating on Cindi. "I understand I have you to thank for that unexpected visit, as a matter of fact."

She shrugged. "Well, I knew something wasn't right. Robin has been moping around since we got back from the cruise." She glanced at Robin with a grin. "You sly little devil. You never hinted that anything improper went on while you were with him...and yet you spend the night with him as soon as he appears, which I find very, very interesting.''

''What did you do?'' Robin asked Cindi hoarsely. ''Did you tell my brothers about—'' Her throat clogged up and she couldn't say another word, but the horrifying picture was beginning to form in her mind.

''I just gave his card to Josh, that's all. I told him not to tell you because you didn't know I saw that you'd tossed it. With you moping around, acting so strange and all it was only natural that we'd be worried about you....'' She looked from Steve to Robin to Steve. ''What's wrong? Isn't everything worked out between you?''

Steve nodded. ''We're getting married, if that's what you mean.''

Robin spun around and looked at him. ''My brothers came to see you?''

He nodded, watching her with more than a hint of wariness.

''When?''

''Day before yesterday.''

''You came to Austin the day after they came to visit you?''

''Actually, Jason flew out there. So I hitched a ride back with them yesterday.''

Robin turned on her heel and walked away from them. She stood with her back to them, trying desperately to gain control over the clash of emotions she was feeling at the moment. After several deep, calming breaths, she slowly revolved to face Steve.

''I can't believe this,'' she said. ''This is absolutely absurd. My brothers hauled you back to Austin to...to what? Force you to marry me?'' She looked at Cindi. ''I thought you were my friend, and yet you went behind my back and deliberately talked to my brothers about what happened when you knew my feelings on the matter? You told them about Steve? And not only that, you actually helped them discover where he lived?''

Cindi folded her arms across her chest and glared at Robin. ''Well, it's obvious to me that *you* haven't been all that honest with me, Robin. I believed you when you said nothing happened while you were on the island. Remember? He was a perfect gentleman, you said...you shared a few kisses, but that's all. And I believed you. I always believe you, Robin. I've never had any reason to doubt your word.

''When Josh came to me and asked me what was wrong with you, I told him I didn't know. We talked about all the possibilities—your classes, your health, the trip we took. I mentioned that you'd met a man, and of course he wanted to know all the details.'' She shrugged her shoulders. ''Okay. So I knew you didn't want the family to know that you missed part of the cruise, but, Robin, you've got to understand that we've all been really worried about you. I figured if there was even the slightest chance that whatever was bothering you had to do with this guy, the family should find out more about him.

''So, in answer to your accusations—yes, I gave Josh the card, and yes, I knew they would probably contact him, even if it made you furious. We felt it was important enough to take some heat over. Obviously it was, because he's here. You're going to marry him. What are you so upset about?''

For a brief time Robin thought she was going to throw up. Never had she felt so much betrayal by so many of the people that she loved and trusted. She'd told her brothers exactly how she felt about their overprotectiveness and they had as good as given their word that they would stay out of her social life from now on. She had trusted them, just as she had trusted Cindi to keep the confidences she'd shared with her to herself.

Trust.

She faced Steve. "You didn't come to Austin to see why I gave you a wrong number, did you? You came because my brothers gave you no alternative."

Steve shook his head. "Don't make a big deal out of this, okay? When they told me of their concern, I wanted to see you, to make sure you were all right. I owe them a debt of gratitude. If they hadn't showed up, I might never have—"

"Oh, I get the picture," she said, pressing her hand against her stomach, praying she wouldn't disgrace herself. "I definitely understand. I would never have heard from you again. I should be thrilled that my brothers once again bulldozed their way into my affairs in order to take care of me."

"They love you," Steve said quietly. He paused, then added softly, "As do I."

Men! She couldn't believe their simple way of looking at things. If they couldn't fight it, eat it, ride it or make love to it, they were unable to relate to a situation.

She just bet that Steve hit it off with her brothers. Why, she couldn't have picked anyone more like one of them. It's a wonder all their swaggering egos could fit into one room. Why hadn't she seen that before now?

Robin glanced at her watch. "I've got to get ready for class." She looked at Steve. "And you need to get back to work."

"I'm not leaving until we get this straightened out, Robin. I know you're upset and—"

"You're darned right I'm upset. So let me just

straighten all of this out for you...and for my brothers. Thank you for your marriage proposal, even though you had a metaphorical shotgun at your back. You've proved that you're an honorable man. However, I'm going to say no to your generous offer. Upon further reflection, marriage is the last thing I want in my life. I'm sick and tired of everyone deciding behind my back what's best for me and how I need to be taken care of. You can tell my brothers that you made your offer, but I refused. Okay? I refuse your gentlemanly, courtly offer of marriage to save my so-called good name. Goodbye, Steve.''

She turned and followed the sidewalk up to the front door of the apartment building without looking back. She figured that Cindi would find a way to console Steve.

Cindi. Her best friend.

Her ex-best friend.

Well, she could have him for all she cared. Italian stallion, indeed.

All Robin's fears had coalesced into the realization that marrying Steve would be like going to prison. Oh, he would be tender and caring and oh, so loving, but he would make certain that she was insulated and cared for, just as her brothers had done. It would be worse than having her brothers hanging around. A husband would have a right to be protective, more so than her brothers.

It would drive her crazy,

No. She'd had a very close call. Thank God she'd found out the truth behind his unexpected appearance before she started making plans for a future together.

She was very lucky. She kept wiping the tears off her cheeks as she entered the apartment. ''I'm not crying because of him,'' she muttered to the empty rooms. ''I'm crying because I'm angry. That's all. But I'll get over it.''

She went to her room and changed into fresh clothing, then headed off to class, aware that Cindi and Steve, along with his rental car, were gone. At the moment she sincerely hoped she never saw either of them again.

"Mom?" Robin said into the phone late that night. "I was wondering if I could come home for a few days? I need to talk to you."

"Why, honey, you don't have to ask for permission to come home. We're always thrilled to have you. But won't you be missing several classes? What's up?"

"I'd, uh, I'd rather wait until I get home to talk, okay?"

"I have an idea. Rather than you coming here, why don't your dad and I come to see you? I haven't been to Austin in a while. It would be a nice break from our routine."

"Are you sure? I could just as easily—"

"Actually, the idea is more and more appealing as I consider it. We'll see you tomorrow after your last class, which will be...when?"

"Noon."

"That will work out perfectly. We'll see you then, sweetheart."

"Okay. And...thanks, Mom. I really appreciate it."

Kristi McAlister hung up the phone and turned to her husband. "Something's happened, honey. I've never heard Robin sound like this before. She was trying hard to cover the fact that she was crying. I told her we'd drive to Austin tomorrow to see her."

Jason looked at her from around the newspaper he was reading. "What's wrong?"

"She wouldn't say."

He removed his reading glasses from his nose. ''You suppose the boys have done something?''

Kristi looked at her husband and grinned. ''I wouldn't want to put money against that being the case.''

He sighed. ''Me, neither.'' He pushed himself out of his leather recliner and strode down the hall to his office. ''I'll get a hold of Jase and see what I can find out from him,'' he said over his shoulder.

Kristi picked up the book she'd been reading when the phone rang, but somehow couldn't get back into the story.

She'd worried about Robin ever since it became obvious that she would be the only girl in the family. Jason always said that Robin was the spitting image of her mother. What Kristi had worried about was her sensitivity and vulnerability, which she'd carefully concealed from her father and three rather overbearing brothers. Robin had learned early to stand up to them and to make them back off. Kristi smiled at the memory of a tiny Robin, before she'd started school, sitting on top of Jim and pulling his hair because he'd been teasing her.

Yes, Robin had grown up scrapping with her brothers, as competitive as they were, attempting to be as strong and as tough. That had worked out fairly well until she became a teenager and it became obvious to her brothers that Robin was strikingly beautiful and attracted every male eye that spotted her.

Kristi had felt better that Robin had her brothers to look out for her. She knew Robin had chafed at their clumsy efforts, but Kristi had hoped her reassurances over the years that Robin's brothers looked out for her because of their love for her would mitigate some of Robin's wounded feelings. The truth was that Robin needed a little protecting from a rather harsh world. Her tender heart could be bruised so easily.

When Jason walked back into the room, he looked pale beneath his deep tan. She jumped up. "Dear Lord, what's wrong!" He wrapped his arm around her waist and sat down on the sofa, pulling her into his lap. "It's bad, isn't it?" she asked with motherly apprehension.

He nodded, then hugged her to him for the longest while without saying a word. Finally he said, "Honey, I know you want to see Robin, but I think maybe we should let me go and talk with her."

"What *is* it! What have the boys done now?"

Jason loved his wife with a passionate intensity that hadn't abated through the many years of marriage and child rearing. He knew his sons had gotten their protective tendencies from watching his attitude toward Kristi and his family. How could he fault them for doing what he'd always done? He didn't want to bring Kristi pain, but he knew that what he had to say would be hard for her to hear.

"Robin wasn't completely up front with us about her cruise, honey," he finally said.

She lifted her head from his chest. "What do you mean?"

He looked into her large, wide-set eyes that had always had the same effect on him since she'd been a baby. "Nothing to get excited about. I don't think. But the fact is that Jase believes, and I tend to agree with him, that Robin had a romantic interlude while she was gone. As soon as he heard about it, Jason and the boys checked the guy out. He lives in Los Angeles, he's a detective with the police force there, and he seems to be a nice enough guy. He also appears to be genuinely in love with Robin, or so Jase thinks."

"I can't believe this! And she didn't tell us a word about meeting a man."

He sighed heavily. "I know. That's what bothers me about this. I want to talk to her—about the fact that she kept this from us, the fact that she called Jase today and said that as far as she's concerned she no longer has any brothers—"

"Oh, no!" Kristi said. "I know she gets angry at them, but she's never threatened to dismiss them from her life."

"Well, that's what she did today. I may be wrong, but I think that if you're there, she'll hide behind you and not talk with me about the situation. I need to get her to deal with this and not to hide behind her mother."

Kristi shook her head in dismay. "But, Jason, I told her we'd both be there. Why don't I go to Austin with you, and let you talk to her first? Eventually she's going to want to talk to me, and I want to be there for her."

"I suppose that will work. Jase thinks these two spent several nights alone together. In fact, he's certain of the facts, just not sure how much of that time they were actually, uh, together, if you follow me."

"She made love to him."

Her bald statement made him flinch. "Yeah," he drawled. "That's what it looks like."

"Did the man admit to it?"

"Let's say he didn't deny it. He also said that he wanted to marry Robin."

"In that case, there shouldn't be a problem."

"So it would seem. Then why is Robin upset? Shouldn't she be happy if she's fallen in love? There's something here I don't like. We'll go see her tomorrow and find out what's going on."

Cindi opened the door of the apartment the next morning in response to Robin's father's knock. Her eyes widened when she saw him. "Well, hi, Papa Mac, what are *you* doing here?"

"Robin wanted to talk with us, so mom and I drove here to see her. Kristi wanted to do some shopping first, so she dropped me off here."

Cindi looked like hell, Jason thought. "So what's going on?"

She shook her head. "I really can't talk about it. I've already done enough damage," she said wearily. "Robin's moving out as soon as she can find another place. She's made it clear she no longer wants me in her life."

He frowned. "What nonsense. You two are closer than sisters."

"Well, she said I overstepped the boundaries this time." She sat down in one of the chairs and motioned for Jason to do the same. "I've got to admit she may be right. I thought I was doing the right thing at the time, but all I've done is really mess up everything!"

"Is this about that man in L.A.?"

Cindi's eyes widened in alarm. "Oh, my gosh! How did you hear about him?"

"Is it?"

"Partly...well, mostly...and the fact that she said I betrayed her trust."

"Because you told Josh about him?"

She rubbed her hands across her face. "Yeah. I've never done anything like that before, but I was so *worried* about her. Now she just wants me out of her life." She glanced at her watch. "I've got to go. She'll be here in a few minutes. It will be better if I stay out of the way." She got up. "I'm really sorry all of this worked out so badly. I hope she'll forgive me. Eventually."

Jason waited another fifteen minutes after Cindi left before he heard Robin's key in the door. He stood and waited for her to come inside.

She looked like hell. Her eyes were red and swollen. She was much too pale, and as soon as she saw him she burst into tears. In two strides he was beside her and holding her tightly against his chest.

"Having a rough time of it, little sister?" he murmured, rubbing her back soothingly.

They stood that way for uncounted minutes until Robin finally pulled away, wiping her cheeks with her hands. "I'm sorry, Dad. I don't know what's the matter with me." She looked around. "Where's Mom?"

"She had a couple of errands to run, so I told her to drop me off here so we could visit."

Robin turned away. "How about a sandwich? Maybe a cup of coffee?"

He had a hunch she hadn't eaten in a while. Jason ignored the fact that he'd eaten less than an hour ago and said, "Sure, sounds fine to me."

He watched his graceful, enchanting daughter as she quickly put on coffee and made sandwiches, marveling that he could be the father to such a beautiful woman. She was her mother all over again—generous and impulsive and warm and loving. His heart ached because he knew he couldn't protect her from the pain she was presently feeling.

Jason made certain that she ate, keeping her entertained during the meal with stories about the ranch and the antics of her silly cat that had taken over the household after her owner had gone off to college. He actually managed to get a smile out of her a couple of times.

Once they were finished eating, Jason leaned back in his chair and said, "Want to tell me about it?"

She looked uncomfortable. "Well, actually, I was hoping to talk to Mom about this."

"Uh-huh. You think your old dad might be a little upset with you?"

She eyed him uncertainly, then made a face. "You've talked to Jase, haven't you?"

"If I had, would that make a difference?"

"Men just don't understand," she finally said.

"What is it we don't understand?" he said, determined not to show his amusement at her obvious frustration.

"I'm barely twenty-two. Almost out of college. But I've never been on my own. Even going away for college didn't help. I've always had brothers around, even here."

"So you're angry at your brothers."

"I'm tired of their interference in my life."

"Do you think your mother and I interfere too much?"

"Not really. You're just very protective, that's all."

"We love you."

"I know you do. But sometimes I feel suffocated by all the attention. I hate that everything I do has to be vetted and commented on by my family."

"*You* called *us,* remember? That's why I'm here. What is it you need from us?"

"Your moral support. That's all. I've accepted a position at the company where I worked last summer. I'm going to be working part-time for the rest of the semester. I intend to find an apartment closer to work. I want my family to understand that I need to do this."

"Okay."

She waited, but he said nothing more. "That's it?" she finally asked.

"If this is what you want, we accept it. You set the boundaries, and we'll abide by them. We want you happy. Believe it or not, honey, that's all we ever wanted.''

She nodded, looking as though she was fighting tears.

''Do you care anything about this man you met while you were on the cruise?''

''Jason *did* tell you about Steve. I knew it!''

He smiled. ''You know, there's really no crime in meeting a man you like, honey. I guess I'm a little surprised that you never bothered to mention him to your mom and me.''

She shrugged. ''There wasn't all that much to tell. I figured it was a typical vacation meeting. Cindi met a guy, too. They've written a couple of cards apiece back and forth, and that will probably be it. It was no big deal.'' She looked down at her hands in her lap. ''Until my brothers got involved and treated it like an international incident. I am so embarrassed. I'll never be able to face him again.''

He straightened and leaned forward. ''Here's the really important thing, sweetheart. Do you want to?''

She stared at him, her misery plain. ''It really doesn't matter anymore, Dad. I made it clear I didn't want him in my life. I don't expect to ever hear from him again.''

Eleven

—

June, Two Years Later

Robin had overslept. The phone woke her a little after ten. As soon as she answered, Don said, ''Where are you? Weren't we playing tennis this morning?''

She sat straight up in bed. ''Oh, no! My alarm didn't go off. Oh, Don. I'm so sorry.''

''We're going to lose the court.'' He sounded disgruntled.

Not that she could blame him. They worked together and had discovered they both enjoyed playing tennis. She had never missed their Saturday-morning tennis match before. Until this morning.

''I'm really sorry, Don. I don't know what happened. Guess we'll have to forget it until next week.''

''Or maybe I'll see if someone's looking for an extra.''

"Good idea. I'll see you Monday."

She hung up the phone, feeling guilty.

Boy, did she ever hate the feeling. She'd dealt with enough guilt and a need for atonement these past couple of years to have earned an eternal state of grace.

She'd almost destroyed her relationship with Cindi.

Whenever she saw her brothers they were distant—treating her so carefully and so awkwardly that she felt like crying with the frustration of it.

Her mother occasionally got a certain look in her eyes that made Robin feel she'd somehow disappointed her, too.

But nothing compared to the rift in the relationship between her and her dad. She'd tried to explain to him several times that she'd just been upset and hurt and angry when she'd leveled so many charges against men in general. She hadn't meant to hurt him.

He'd said at the time that he understood. He'd said that he wanted her to be happy and that he hadn't realized how his attitude, and the attitude of her brothers, had made her so unhappy.

Ever since that day it was as though a wall had grown between her and everyone she loved. They had all stepped back, way back, and politely allowed her to get on with her life.

Her very lonely life.

Of course she'd made friends at work. She'd dated several very nice men in the past couple of years. She enjoyed her job. In fact, Robin now had the life she had dreamed about during her teenage years.

She was free.

She was independent.

She was alone.

It wasn't at all the carefree existence she had expected it to be.

She had no one to blame but herself.

She and Cindi had eventually formed an uneasy truce, mostly because Cindi was never one to harbor a grudge. Robin had found an apartment and moved out before graduation, and Cindi had found another roommate almost immediately. After graduation Cindi had accepted a job in Chicago and rarely came home.

When she *was* home, they got together for lunch to catch up on personal news, but it was not the same.

Nothing was the same.

Cindi had called her three weeks ago to say she'd accepted a ring from the man she'd been dating—Roger something or other. They planned to have a long engagement, but she wanted Robin to be in on the planning of the wedding once they set a date.

It was the *M* word that always set Robin into an emotional spin.

If she hadn't acted like a complete fool way back when, she would be married to Steve Antonelli by now. Instead she'd let her pride take over and she'd shoved him out of her life. She couldn't blame him for not attempting another round with her.

Steve popped into her thoughts once in a while—when she saw a particularly romantic movie or television show, around the holidays, especially Valentine's Day, or when she saw couples obviously enjoying each other.

She wondered if he was married now. Despite what he'd said when they first met about the perils of his profession and a healthy marriage, he'd been willing to take the chance with her. No doubt he had met someone else by now who had been smart enough to say yes.

Robin went in and got her shower, then headed to the

kitchen for coffee. Now that she had no place to go first thing this morning, she would relax with a cup of coffee and the paper before running her weekly errands.

She went to the front door and picked up her paper, then returned to the kitchen. While she waited for the coffee to brew, she flipped through the paper.

On the third page of the news section, she spotted a headline that froze her blood. A gang war in L.A. had wounded several policemen. With trembling hands she read every word. There was no mention of the names of the men who were shot or how badly they were wounded.

With so many police working for the city, the chance of Steve being a part of this particular shooting was very slim. Practically nil.

But her heart continued to pound in her chest. Life was so fragile. How quickly a loved one could be lost.

It was time for her to go to each member of her family and apologize for her behavior. She needed to tell each of them how very much she missed the closeness they once had and how much she wanted it back. Maybe by admitting how wrong she had been she could somehow convince them that she wanted to build a new and stronger relationship.

Tears came to her eyes just thinking about all she needed to say. She loved her family so much, never so much as now when she finally faced and acknowledged to herself that she was responsible for the horrible gulf that had formed between them.

Then she thought of Steve. She always visualized him on the island, wearing shorts...or nothing at all. She'd never really tried to come to terms with what his life must be like at work—the pressure, the stress, the long hours, the frustrations that every law enforcement official had to combat.

He'd once called her a coward, and now she could better understand that he had been right. She'd complained about her life and her brothers like a silly child, while he risked his life daily performing a necessary service in the city where he lived. With the perspective of time, she now knew with complete certainty that if he hadn't wanted to come see her in Austin, there was no way her brothers could have forced the issue.

No one had held a gun to his head when he'd asked her to marry him that night in his hotel room.

What an idiot she had been.

It was at that point in her thinking that Robin suddenly had the idea of going to Los Angeles on her vacation. She had two weeks coming and was scheduled to take the last two weeks of this month. She hadn't made any formal plans. She'd thought to go home for a few days, then maybe down to the coast.

She'd never been to California. What would be wrong if she decided to go out there? Not because Steve was there, of course. He could have moved by now—gotten married, even had a child. No, she would go just to see the place. And if she decided to give him a call while she was there, what could be wrong with that?

Before she had time to talk herself out of it, Robin called her travel agent and booked the trip. Next, she called her parents and told them she wanted to come home to see everyone again.

Three Weeks Later

Robin walked along the Santa Monica sidewalk that overlooked the beach. The weather seemed too good to be true. There was a soft breeze, but the air was cool and the sunshine felt good on her shoulders.

Her travel agent had recommended a hotel in Santa Monica. She was so glad that he had. Her rental car had given her an opportunity to drive around the Los Angeles area, so she had explored both the basin and the valley areas.

She'd gone to Universal Studios one day, visited the observatory, walked the streets of Hollywood, but had always been thankful to return to Santa Monica each afternoon, where she could see the ocean from her hotel window.

She hadn't gotten used to all the flowers blooming everywhere—along the sidewalks, in hanging baskets, in every yard she passed. It was beautiful this time of year. No wonder so many people came to visit southern California and fell in love with the climate.

She had been in California a week now. She'd bought a city map and actually looked up the address that Steve had given her on his card, way back when.

The fact that his phone number and address had been indelibly imprinted into her memory was a little annoying, but in this case it had come in handy. However, now that she was here, she was less and less inclined to actually contact him.

After all, what could she say to him after all this time? He didn't need to hear her admit she'd been a fool where he was concerned. When it came right down to it, they'd known each other less than a week, even counting his visit to Texas. One week. It was silly to think that he would even remember her.

This was one time when her pride would be her salvation. She was pleased she'd come here. She'd enjoyed driving through the hills, finding the famous streets— Sunset Boulevard, Mulholland Drive, as well as looking at all the shops on Rodeo Drive.

There was no reason that she needed to contact the only person she knew in this area on the off chance he might be willing to see her.

Robin crossed the wide boulevard away from the ocean and strolled up one of the main streets, passing shops and restaurants, then residences, and eventually coming to a park with several tennis courts.

What a great place to play, she thought to herself. Too bad she didn't have anyone to play against. Of course, she hadn't brought a racket, but it would be fun to sit and watch for a while before she made the walk back to her hotel.

Robin found an empty bench and sat down.

She wasn't sorry she'd followed her impulse to come out here. That same impulse had caused her to go home the next weekend after she'd booked her flight to California.

As usual, her parents had thrown a party and all her brothers had come.

It was after the party when all of them had been cleaning up that Robin had told them why she'd come home this time.

By the time she'd finished, there hadn't been a dry eye in the place.

Now as she soaked up the California sunshine Robin smiled at the memory of the hugfest that had followed her contrite confession.

It was when her brothers had started to give her all kinds of suggestions and cautioning her about traveling alone in L.A. that she knew she'd been truly forgiven.

She'd solemnly listened to all their advice and when she'd happened to glance over at her dad, he'd winked at her and had given her his very special dad-to-daughter smile that she hadn't seen in a very long while.

She'd known then that she was truly home again.

"Hey, let up a little, will ya?" Ray yelled across the net. "You're killing me with those serves, man."

Steve grinned. "Weren't you the one complaining that I wasn't enough competition for you?"

"Well, yeah, but that was before you signed up for more tennis lessons. You've had me running all over this court. I'm not sure my heart can take it."

"You ready to quit?"

Ray laughed. "Not on your life. Go ahead, give it your best shot!"

They played fast and furiously for several minutes until the game and set were finished.

Steve felt good. His game *had* improved in the past couple of years. He'd also taken up golf, which was a great stress reliever if he didn't take himself too seriously.

There had been a great many changes in his life in the past two years, he was pleased to note. His island vacation had been a time of awakening for him. He'd kept his promise to bring more balance into his life.

Ray joined him by their bags. "Did you see her?"

Steve glanced up from zipping the cover on his racquet. "Who?"

"The redhead seated over there on the bench. I've only seen her profile, but she is one good-looking babe."

Steve didn't look up. "I don't care for redheads," he said.

"Gee, thanks," Ray said, touching his flaming locks. "You really know how to hurt a guy."

"Not you, you idiot."

"Darn, she's leaving. Mm-mm, wish I'd noticed her sooner."

Steve glanced up as the woman who had been outside the fence two courts over from theirs strolled away from them toward the street. There was something about her—about the way she walked, the tilt of her head, her fiery hair tumbling around her shoulders...could it be? No, of course not. He thought he was over his habit of reacting to every tall, slender redhead he spotted. Out here, they were too numerous to mention.

But there was something about this one that seemed so familiar.

Somebody shouted, and she turned and looked back, so she now faced Ray and Steve. She wore sunshades, but when he got a good look at her, he knew he wasn't mistaken. There couldn't be two women like her on the planet.

"Well I'll be damned," he murmured, his hands on his hips.

"Probably, but that's nothing new. What did I tell you? She's really something, isn't she?"

"Hold on, I'll be right back."

Robin had turned back and continued to walk toward the ocean. Because of her leisurely pace, he had no trouble sprinting to catch up with her.

"Robin?" he said, stopping a few feet away from her.

She spun around, looking in several directions, and he was reminded of the time he'd gone to see her on campus. How long ago had that been? In some ways it could have been last week. In others, a lifetime.

He'd thought of her at the time as being naive, when *he'd* been the one dazzled by the stars in his eyes, seduced into believing in happy ever after because of a torrid affair on a tropical island.

She took her sunglasses off and stared at him. He could

just imagine what she was seeing—after two sets of tennis he was hot, sweaty and probably a little aromatic.

"Steve?" she said, her tone one of disbelief. Well, he could certainly relate to that.

"Yeah, it's me. I had to look a couple of times myself when I first spotted you. You're the last person I expected to see here in Santa Monica."

Ray came trotting up behind him. "Don't tell me you actually know her!" he said in disgust. "I can't believe your luck!"

He turned to Ray. "This is Robin McAlister, Ray." He looked back at Robin. "Ray Cassidy is a good friend of mine. It's really weird that you should show up here. We play tennis here a couple of times a week when our schedules permit." He looked around. "Are you here alone?"

She flushed. "Yes, I, uh, came out here on vacation. Today is the first time I've stayed out of the car and traffic. I decided to view the area on foot."

Steve tried not to stare, but damn, she was something to see. She hadn't changed all that much since he'd last seen her. He'd forgotten how beautiful she was. "How long have you been in California?"

"Oh! About a week. I still have another week before I have to go home."

Ray asked, "Where are you from? And do you need a guide? I'll be glad to show you around all the night spots that you might not have seen, if you're on your own."

She smiled, and her dimples flashed. Steve could still feel the same physical response to her he'd always had. Well, he wasn't dead, after all. Any male still breathing would respond to her. Just look at Ray.

"I'm from Texas," she replied.

"Do you need a ride back to your hotel?" Ray asked solicitously. "My car's right over there and I'll be glad to—"

She shook her head, still smiling. "No, thanks. I'm enjoying the exercise." She looked back at Steve. "It's good to see you again. How have you been?"

How had he been? Good question. *You mean, after you broke my heart, trampled my pride and made a complete fool of me? Oh, I've been just great, no thanks to you.*

"Can't complain. So. You're on vacation. Decided against a cruise, did you?"

She laughed, the sound light and so intoxicating he felt as though he could get drunk on it. Damn. He hated the way this particular woman affected him.

"I believe I've had all the experience with a cruise that I can handle."

Ray said, "Is that how you two met? On a cruise?" He looked at Steve. "You never mentioned it."

Steve shrugged. "I wasn't on the cruise. It was a long time ago." He looked at her. "How are your brothers?"

She nodded, as though giving him a point. "My brothers are quite well, thank you."

"Are you enjoying your life? Your job?"

"Yes."

"That's good to hear." He looked at his watch. "Well, it's been great seeing you again. Enjoy your stay in sunny California."

Ray spoke up. "Hey, if you don't have anything planned for this evening, maybe we could get together for dinner." He looked at Steve imploringly.

No. I don't want to see her over dinner. I don't want to spend any more time with this woman. I like my life just fine, thank you very much. She is not going to get to me ever again.

"You mean with both of you?" she asked, showing some confusion.

Ray smiled. "Well, if Steve has other plans, I'd be happy to take you out. Any friend of Steve's is a friend of mine." He touched her hair. "Us redheads need to stick together, you know."

Steve didn't care if Ray took her out. He didn't care what she did or with whom. "Well, actually, I do have plans," he began to say. He watched her expression but couldn't tell what she was thinking. How had he forgotten how green her eyes were? Or the silkiness of her hair and skin? Or the way she had of tilting her head slightly when she was listening? Or the— "But maybe I can rearrange things." He turned to Ray. "Give me a call later and let me know what you worked out. Maybe I can catch up with you at a restaurant."

Steve gave them a wave and walked away.

His heart was pounding so hard in his chest he was afraid he might have a heart attack before he reached the car.

How could this be happening? What sort of sick coincidence would have her strolling by a tennis court where he hung out? He couldn't help but wonder if he would have run into her if he'd been out on the golf course.

Their entire relationship had been a matter of ridiculous circumstances—from her wanting to look at tide pools to slipping and falling trying to get back to the boat.

If this was his guardian angel's idea of fun, Steve was going to petition for another guardian.

He would wait to hear from Ray. Maybe by then, he'd have put together something to keep him busy tonight. He didn't want to see them together. A horrible thought hit him. What if Ray fell for her like any man would? And what if they ended up together? His best friend might end up married to the woman who— The woman who—

Steve decided not to finish that thought. He didn't want to think about it. All right.

The only woman he'd ever wanted to marry; the only woman he'd ever wanted to be the mother of his children; the only woman he'd ever loved.

There. Satisfied? I admitted it. But I'm not doing anything about it. I stuck my neck out and got it chopped off. I much prefer not being in love. It's considerably more comfortable.

And boring, a little voice said.

He ignored that little voice.

Steve's friend seemed very nice. He made her laugh. In fact, he'd insisted on taking Robin back to her hotel so he'd know where to pick her up later.

By the time they reached the hotel, she felt as if she'd known him forever. "Okay," he said, helping her out of the car, "I'll see you tonight, about seven-thirty or so. I can't believe my luck, running into an acquaintance of Steve's like this. I hope you'll let me be your guide for the rest of your stay."

She pulled her hand out of his grasp with a smile. "We'll see, Ray. I enjoyed meeting you. I'll see you tonight, okay?" She turned and walked into the hotel.

She made it all the way to her room before her knees gave way.

How could this be? She wondered, limply sinking onto her bed. How could she have run into Steve Antonelli out of all the people who lived in southern California?

Had he mentioned to her that he played tennis in Santa Monica when they'd first met?

She couldn't remember. He'd told her he didn't live far from the beach and that he intended to spend more time there once he returned home. His condominium was located in West Los Angeles, so it wasn't too far-fetched to think he might visit this area. It was possible that on some level she'd known that and had made her plans accordingly.

So now she was committed to having dinner with his friend, Ray. She liked Ray, but she was a little afraid he was hoping for a closer relationship than she was willing to consider. That was all that she would need—to date a friend of Steve's, like some lovelorn adolescent pining for the guy she could never get and hanging around the fringes of his life.

It didn't help to remind herself that there had been a time when she could have been a part of Steve's life. Even though she'd known how rare love was, even though she'd known that what she felt was the real thing, she'd been too caught up in her battle with her brothers to appreciate all that Steve meant in her life.

No, she hadn't grown up with him next door, but that didn't make what had happened between them any less real.

She wondered if it would do any good for her to tell him how she felt. Would it change anything? Even if his feelings had changed, didn't she want him to know how much she regretted the way things ended between them?

She would leave it up to fate. She might not see him tonight. He certainly had made no effort to find out where she was staying, making it clear that he had no intention of following up on their meeting. So maybe he wouldn't come tonight.

Her discussion with her family had been successful. Maybe if she spoke to Steve, explained all that she had faced during these past two years, maybe— She didn't want to think about how he might respond, but the outcome could be as positive as her meeting with her family. And wouldn't that be a wonderful conclusion to her visit?

She could only play the cards that had been dealt to her.

Robin was suitably impressed when they pulled up in front of a restaurant that she'd only read about as being a hangout for the stars. Ray turned the keys over to the valet attendant and escorted her inside.

She heard him say they had reservations for four, which surprised her. If Steve was planning to meet them, he obviously wasn't coming alone.

Once they were seated and gave their drink orders, she asked, "I forgot to ask, is Steve married now?"

Ray laughed. "No way. He has no intention of getting married. Not with his job."

She nodded. "Yes, he'd mentioned his concerns about that when we met. I just wondered, since you said there were four for dinner."

Ray shrugged. "Well, when I finally ran him down this afternoon, he said he'd meet us for dinner and he'd bring his date. I don't know who, but if you know Steve at all, you know there's generally a line of women waiting to get his attention."

The waiter returned with their drinks, so Robin didn't have to respond. She wasn't certain she could have, even if her life depended on it.

Steve with a date.

The thought hit her like a blow to her solar plexus, taking her breath away.

Well, she'd wanted to know what had happened to him, hadn't she? She'd come to California with the idea of looking him up and then lost her courage, which was nothing new.

So now she would have the opportunity to see him in his own element. Maybe after this she would be able to erase him from her memory and stop comparing every man she met with her memory of him.

"Ah, here they come," Ray said, leaning over and speaking into her ear. "As usual, he's found him a hot one."

Indeed he had. The woman walking in front of Steve as they threaded their way through the tables was everything that Robin wasn't. For starters, she was petite with a curvaceous figure shown to advantage in the short black dress with a deep V neckline.

Her ivory skin was in stark contrast to her dark eyes and black curly hair worn long. When Ray stood to greet them, Robin expected his tongue to hit the floor.

She really couldn't blame him. The woman was stunning, there was no other word to describe her.

When they reached the table, Steve casually draped his arm across the woman's shoulders. "Tricia, this is my friend, Ray, and this is Robin, visiting our fair state from Texas."

Tricia smiled at them both. "Hello," she said, and sat in the chair Steve pulled out for her.

Robin felt as though she were in some kind of nightmare and hoped that she would awaken soon. She tried to keep up with the conversation, but it was difficult. All she could do was notice how Steve treated Tricia—the way he once acted toward her.

Steve was a toucher—and it was obvious that he felt comfortable touching Tricia.

Ray seemed to be enamored of her, as well. What was there not to like, after all? The woman had a husky, seductive voice that seemed to draw people closer to her, as though they were afraid to miss even a word.

What was worse, despite her sultry good looks, Tricia was a nice person. She didn't put on airs. In fact, she seemed to be totally unaware of her effect on the men at the table, as well as the ones in the restaurant who kept glancing at their table.

As dinner progressed Robin knew that had she met this woman under any other circumstances, she would have really liked her. But the melting glances she kept giving Steve, the familiar way she had of speaking to him, touching his arm and hand, the way she sparkled as she teased him, made it clear that Robin didn't stand a chance to gain even a small part of Steve's attention tonight.

To think that she'd considered telling him how much she still cared for him. Thank God she'd been treated to this exhibition of mutual admiration before she'd spilled her innermost feelings to him.

"I have a great idea," Ray said over dessert and coffee. "Let's go dancing and show these women off. What do you say, Steve?"

Steve's gaze went to Tricia in a silent query. She gave him a mischievous smile and stroked his shoulder. "I'd love it," she said.

"You sure?" he asked doubtfully.

"Positive," she replied with a breathy laugh. "I'm having a wonderful time."

Robin forced a smile on her face. "That sounds like fun," she said, lying through her teeth.

She had no one else to blame but herself for the following hours of hell watching Steve and Tricia as they performed a great many Latin dances as though they'd danced together for years. He'd never mentioned to her that he liked to dance, that he had impeccable timing and a grace that made her remember his lovemaking like a hollow ache in the pit of her stomach.

Ray was no slouch on the dance floor, himself. Robin had been shy about trying some of the dances, but he was so good at leading, that she quickly became comfortable following his direction.

No matter how horrifying a nightmare might be, eventually it has to come to an end, and this evening was no exception. They would be leaving soon. Ray to return her to her hotel. Steve to take his companion home.

"I think I'll visit the ladies' room before we leave," Tricia said when they'd returned to the table after the band took a break. She looked at Robin. "How about you?"

Robin nodded. "Good idea," she said, picking up her purse. She followed Tricia into the elaborate lounge and through to the facilities. When Robin returned to the lounge area she sat down in front of the mirror and pulled a comb from her purse.

She felt like a giant around Tricia, and when Tricia sat in the chair next to her, the contrast between them was almost laughably obvious. She watched with a rather morbid fascination as Tricia took a tube of lipstick out of her purse, then carefully outlined her full and sultry mouth.

Robin had an immediate vision of Steve's mouth devouring Tricia's luscious lips. She swallowed and looked away.

"This has been so much fun," Tricia said, putting the lipstick away and quickly pulling a comb through her long hair. "I'm so glad I was able to come."

"I enjoyed meeting you," Robin said, determined to

be polite if it killed her. "You and Steve look really good together out on the dance floor. I'm very impressed."

Tricia laughed. "Oh, he can be such a show-off at times, but I love him, anyway."

Who can blame her?

"I should feel guilty for leaving Danny with Paul tonight, but when Steve called with the invitation, Paul insisted I deserved to get out for a few hours and have some fun. He offered to stay home with Danny so I wouldn't worry about him. That's the trouble with staying home all the time with a two-year-old, pretty soon you forget there's any other life out there."

Robin blinked. "I'm sorry, I'm afraid I don't understand. You have a two-year-old?"

Tricia nodded, her eyes shining. "Yes. He's the light of our lives."

"You and Steve?" she managed to say, unable to hide the quaver in her voice.

Tricia looked at her, obviously perplexed by the question. With a slight frown, she asked, "Are you serious? Didn't Steve tell you who I am?"

"Well, no. Ray just told me that Steve was bringing a date tonight."

Tricia burst into delighted laughter. "A date! Oh, wait until I tell Paul! He's going to laugh his fool head off. This is priceless." She reached over and patted Robin's hand. "I can't believe that nobody mentioned it to you. I'm married to Paul Anderson....

"Steve is my brother."

Twelve

"Steve Antonelli is your *brother?*" Her voice sounded shrill to Robin's ears, but she couldn't help it. After the evening she'd been through, she felt as though she'd gone into shock.

Tricia nodded slowly, obviously puzzled by Robin's reaction.

"I had no idea!"

"Well, he probably didn't want to make a big deal out of it. I'm sure he wouldn't want you to think that he couldn't get a date or something."

"The thought would never occur to me."

"I probably shouldn't even mention this, and I want you to promise not to let on that I said anything, but Steve got hurt pretty badly a couple of years ago, and he's practically stopped dating entirely. That's one reason Paul insisted I go with him tonight. We were pleased that he was at least willing to get out and socialize a little."

Robin didn't know what to say. Too much information had been thrown at her too fast, and her head was spinning.

"I never did hear the details, but from snippets of various remarks I've heard in the family, Steve met this woman while he was on vacation and fell head over heels in love with her. Family rumor has it he was prepared to chuck his job and move to wherever she was from. But she must have turned him down. It's too bad, because I think Steve would make the greatest husband and father. He's wonderful with Danny. Whatever happened, it changed him. He seems to have lost his drive. Of course, Dad thinks the change is for the better. He's not so obsessed with his job, and he spends much more time with the family." She laughed. "He's even taken up golf. But whenever I ask if he's dating anyone, he just shrugs and says he hasn't met anyone that interests him. It just breaks my heart."

"Yes," Robin replied slowly. "That *is* heartbreaking."

Tricia hopped up. "The guys are going to be wondering what happened to us."

They walked back into the club and found the men talking. Once again Steve gave Tricia a loving look, touching her hand with obvious affection. *His sister.* No wonder there was such an obvious bond between them and they danced so well together.

Oh, Steve. I hate it that you've been hurting. I want so much to make it up to you if you'd only let me.

The couples said goodbye while they waited for their cars to be brought around by the valet service.

"It was nice seeing you again, Robin," Steve said without meeting her eyes. "Tell your family hello for me."

Ray took her arm, waved to Steve and Tricia and helped Robin into the car.

"You're awfully quiet," he said as they made their way through traffic.

"Just tired. Remember I'm still working on Central Standard Time, so it's two hours later to me than it is you."

"Ouch. Well, I'll forgive you this time. Now, about tomorrow—"

He paused and glanced over at her expectantly.

"I'll probably spend half the day asleep."

"I was serious about being your guide while you're in town, Robin. I would really like to get to know you better."

"That's very sweet of you, Ray, but I don't want to give you the wrong idea."

"There's somebody else," he said with comic woe.

She nodded.

"Of course there is. No one in his right mind would let you walk away. But a guy can dream."

"I had a great time tonight. I appreciate all that you've done."

"Hey, it was my pleasure. Every moment of it. And if you want a guide, I'm still available, no strings attached."

She reached over and touched his hand that rested against the steering wheel. "Thank you for that."

Robin had him leave her in front of the hotel, then went upstairs to her room. She had to decide what to do next. She hadn't lied, she really was tired, but she also knew that she was too keyed-up to be able to sleep.

She had no idea how long it would take Steve to get Tricia home, but after pacing the floor for several minutes, Robin changed out of her evening wear and into a pair of comfortable jeans and a sweater. The night air here was always cool, something she appreciated after spending so many summers in Texas.

She returned downstairs, went to her rental car and drove to the address she'd carried in her head for the past two years.

When she arrived, the place was dark. She pulled in across the street and parked. She would wait for him. She'd rather be here than tossing and turning in bed.

About twenty minutes later headlights appeared at the end of the street, coming toward her. The car slowed, then pulled into the condo unit where Steve lived. She watched as the garage door swung open, he pulled in and the door shut.

She waited a few minutes as various lights went on, signaling his path through the place. When she felt she'd given him enough time to settle in without getting ready for bed, Robin walked to the front door and rang the bell.

She couldn't help but wonder if he would open the door once he saw her through the security peephole. Her question was answered when she heard the door being unlocked.

"What in the world are you doing here at this time of night?" he asked when he faced her.

"I was hoping to be able to speak with you."

"Now?" He stepped back and motioned for her to come inside.

He'd removed his sports jacket and shoes. His shirt was unbuttoned and hanging open. She'd almost waited too long.

He led her into a well-furnished living room and waved his arm. "Have a seat."

She sat on the sofa. He sat across the room from her in an overstuffed chair.

"You once called me a coward," she began.

"Did I? I don't recall."

"And you were right."

"And that's what you came to tell me?"

"Partly. Because the reason I took my vacation and came out here was to find you, to talk with you and to tell you some things. The problem was that once I got here I didn't have the courage to go through with it. I had made up my mind not to seek you out when we ran into each other today."

He shrugged. "Obviously kismet, right?"

She hated his bored expression and tone. But she understood it so much better than she had before. He'd been hurt very badly. His attitude was the best way he knew to defend himself from further hurt.

"It's hard for me to find the words to explain. There's so much I want to say. The most important thing is to tell you how sorry I am."

"For what?"

"For not honoring the strength of my feelings for you. For taking your feelings for me so lightly. Everything happened so fast between us. I was totally unprepared."

"I believe that we've already had this conversation, Robin. It's really late, and I'm bushed." He'd rested his ankle on his knee and kept wiggling his foot as though keeping time to music only he could hear.

She was thankful that he hadn't turned on a light here in the living room. The hall light left the room in shadows. If she kept her voice steady enough, she hoped he wouldn't be able to see the tears that were trickling down her cheeks.

"I needed some time to grow up," she went on, as though he hadn't spoken. "To get my priorities straight.

To decide what and who I wanted to be when I grew up.''

He stilled, as though suddenly frozen.

''I got the job I wanted. I gained the freedom from my family I wanted. In fact, everything I'd looked forward to once I graduated came to pass. I was very fortunate in that respect. That's when I realized that none of that was important to me anymore without you in my life.''

''Why are you here?'' Steve asked hoarsely, his face concealed by the shadows.

''I wanted to tell you that I never stopped loving you, Steve. Not from the first time we met. I wasn't ready for the shock of meeting the love of my life at that time and I didn't handle it well. The depth of my feelings for you scared me to death. I've never felt so vulnerable, nor have I ever been so ill equipped to handle such an emotional situation. I can never take away the harsh words I spoke to you, the thoughtless cruelty of my actions. I couldn't truly comprehend that you might love me in the same way. That what we had was a once-in-a-lifetime thing that some people never find.

''I came out here because I wanted to find out if you'd found happiness since I last saw you. If you'd found the fulfillment you deserve, because that's what I wish for you—all the love, the joy and the fulfillment that you deserve.''

He sat there without moving.

She waited, but he didn't say a word. The silence grew and stretched and eventually filled the room. There was nothing more to say. She didn't want him to hear how close she was to losing complete control. Another word and her voice would crack.

Without a word she got up and walked out of the room. The silence in the condo was excruciatingly painful, but she refused to be sorry for coming to him tonight. The relief of getting all of that off her chest was tremendously freeing.

Robin let herself out of the condo, walked to the car and drove away.

She had hoped that he might still have some feeling for her, some positive feeling, that is. She had hoped he would be able to forgive her for her lack of maturity when they first met.

Until now, she hadn't been aware how strong her expectations had been that he might accept her apology...until none of them were met.

Maybe it was because her family had been so open to her apologies and willing to forgive her, that she had hoped Steve might be willing to forgive her as well.

She had been so wrong. The knowledge was devastating. What had she done to this strong, independent, yet warm and loving man when she'd changed her mind about marrying him?

How could she have turned her back on the love he had offered her so freely? She'd been so caught up in her little girl hurt that she'd been unable to focus on anything other than her own pain. She'd never once given a thought to what her rejection had done to him.

Now she had to live with what she had done...to both of them. He'd made it clear tonight that he wanted nothing more to do with her.

She couldn't blame him in the slightest. No doubt it would have been easier to forgive herself if she had received some kind of absolution from him.

Too bad that life seldom worked out the way we hoped and planned.

Robin knew as she drove back to her hotel that she had gotten exactly what she deserved.

Somehow, some way, she would have to live with the knowledge for the rest of her life that she'd destroyed what could have been a strong and loving relationship with the man who would always hold her heart in his very capable hands.

By the time she reached the hotel garage, Robin was grateful she didn't have to go through the lobby. She found tissues in her purse, wiped her eyes and blew her nose, then went up to her room once again.

It was almost three o'clock in the morning. Not only the lateness of the hour and the different time zone but the emotional trial she'd faced tonight...and lost...had taken their toll.

She fell into a deep sleep, too emotionally drained to think about what the rest of her life would be like without Steve as part of it.

Thirteen

The pounding in her head refused to go away.

Robin groaned and rolled over in bed. She hadn't drunk enough the night before to have this severe a hangover. She forced her eyes open to look at the clock. Six o'clock. She'd barely had three hours of sleep.

The pounding continued.

Only then did she realize it was someone monotonously rapping on her door. She fumbled for her robe and drew it around her, then went to the door and peered through the security viewer.

Hurriedly she unhooked the chain, twisted the lock and opened the door.

He looked awful—unshaven, his hair standing out in all directions, his shirt rumpled, his slacks hopelessly creased and a ferocious scowl on his face.

Silently she stepped back and motioned for him to come inside, then closed the door behind him. She turned and leaned against the door, watching him, waiting for she knew not what.

He swayed on his feet, whether from alcohol or exhaustion she did not know. But he had come to her. He was here…and her heart felt as though it wanted to leap out of her chest.

When he spoke, his voice was harsh and angry. "Damn you!"

Then he grabbed her and wrapped his arms around her as though he never intended to let go. She closed her eyes, buried her head in his shoulder and held him with equal strength.

They stood like that forever, it seemed. Robin couldn't get close enough to him. She wanted to touch him everywhere, to love him in every way she knew how and to take away the hurt she'd unintentionally inflicted.

She had never loved anyone with this much intensity. She felt as though she might burst with the pressure of her feelings for him.

"I was over you," he said in that same guttural voice, as though he was forcing the words through a raw throat. "I'd gotten through the worst of it. I'd grown grateful for the fact that we lived too far from each other to ever accidentally see you. And then, there you were, as though you'd sprung into being from a figment of my imagination."

She held on to him, her arms aching with the tension of holding him so tightly. "I love you, Steve. I love you so much," she whispered.

"You put me through hell," he said, his words sounding like a groan.

"I didn't mean to. I never meant to hurt you. Please believe that."

"I vowed never to ask you to marry me again. Never! I will never put myself through that again."

She squeezed her eyes shut, trying to absorb his pain. "It's okay," she whispered. "It's going to be okay. We'll work it out. I promise."

She felt his knees sag just as she got him to the bed. They tumbled onto the bed, their arms still around each other. "I'm so tired," he said. "I'm tired of fighting what I feel. So tired of denying it to myself. Tired of pretending everything is all right in my life when there's so little there."

"It will be different. I promise. I'll move out here. We'll see each other as often as you want. I'll get a job. This is the public relations Mecca of the world. I won't starve. We'll take our time and rebuild the trust. Just know I love you. I always will."

In moments he was asleep, clutching her to him. Robin relaxed and fell back to sleep, as exhausted as he was. She had no idea how long she slept, but when she awoke, she was alone.

Robin sat up in bed. Had she dreamed that Steve had come to her? She looked at the clock. It was after three in the afternoon and it was raining.

Only then did she register that there was bright sunlight peeking around her drawn drapes. The sound of rain she heard was the shower.

She hurried across the room and opened the bathroom door. The room was steamy, the mirror misted. Robin pulled off her nightshirt and stepped into the shower, wrapping her arms around the naked man standing under the spray of water.

"Hi," she said, placing a kiss on his bristly chin.

He looked down at her with an expression of wonderment. "Hi, yourself."

He reached up and pushed his hair out of his eyes. "You're real. I keep thinking I'm just making all of this up."

"I know what you mean." She turned him around, then lathered his back, enjoying the feel of the muscles along his spine and shoulders. And that taut butt of his, the only part of him that was pale, tempted her to stroke and squeeze as well.

When he turned back to her, he was fully aroused.

"Well, hello there," she said, stroking his length. The reaction was immediate.

He soaped her body quickly, efficiently and with obvious intent not to prolong the process. When he turned off the water, she stepped out and grabbed a towel, tossed it to him and used another to dry herself.

She was trying to towel her hair dry when he opened the door and pulled her behind him back to the bed.

Their lovemaking was fierce, intense and shattering. No words were spoken, but their love for each other was revealed in so many ways. By the time he collapsed on top of her, they were both sobbing for breath and with emotion.

He held her to him, even after he shifted his weight to lie beside her. "Don't ever leave me," he whispered. "I couldn't stand it."

"Neither could I," she whispered in response.

She lost track of time. The next time she stirred it was because Steve muttered something obscene just under his breath.

"What is it?"

"I was supposed to be at work an hour ago."

"Oh, no. What are you going to do?"

He sat up and reached for the phone. "I'll have to tell them there was a family emergency that I had to handle."

He reached for her hand. "I'll say that something came up," he wrapped her fingers around his rapidly enlarging flesh, "and that a friend is helping me deal with it."

"A friend?"

"A very close friend."

She listened as he talked to his superior. When he hung up, he turned back to her, kissing and caressing her until she reached a fevered pitch before he took her once again.

"I've missed you," he said, his rhythm slow and steady, "and I've missed making love to you like this."

"This may not be the time to mention this," she said, meeting each thrust with her own.

"What?"

"I need to pick the proper time and place," she added, panting.

"Tell me," he said.

"Ask you," she corrected.

"Whatever."

"Steve, my only love, will you marry me?"

He stared down at her, his rhythm forgotten. "What did you say?"

"You said you would never ask me to marry you again. I understand and appreciate your point. But since we've made no effort to use any type of birth control, it seems to me that we need to consider the possible consequences. I know I'm being quite bold, but—"

His mouth covered hers, and she lost her train of thought. Not that she was too worried. She might not get the desired answer right away, but if all else failed, she could put in a call to her brothers.

They were excellent at ferreting out marriage prey.

Epilogue

October, Same Year

Ray tapped Robin on the shoulder. When she turned around, he swept her into his arms and gave her a leisurely kiss.

"You like to live dangerously?" Steve asked his friend. He was not smiling.

Ray ignored him until he was finished. Then he slowly let go of her and smiled with angelic sweetness. "It's a long-held tradition that the best man always gets to kiss the bride, Steve." He winked at Robin. "I'm sure that your brand-new wife is well aware that I *am* the best man. You're the consolation prize. Just the breaks of the game, I'm afraid."

Robin laughed as Steve slipped a proprietary arm around her waist and hugged her close to his side.

"All right. One kiss. Don't think you can get away with another one."

The reception at the ranch was in full swing. Her dad had always been able to throw a festive party and this one was no exception. The place was crowded with all kinds of relatives and friends from both families.

The California contingent had been coming in for the last week. Steve's mom and dad had come early so they could become acquainted with her family.

Of course, she had already met them back in June during her vacation. She would always treasure the memories of that last week she'd spent with Steve.

She had moved in with him for the remainder of her stay. He managed to get a couple more days off work so they were able to go to Santa Barbara for her to meet Tony and Susan. She'd immediately fallen in love with Steve's parents.

Over dinner with them that evening, she'd regaled them with the story of Steve taking his sister out on a double date without bothering to mention their relationship.

"Obviously he wanted to make me jealous," she concluded, as everyone at the table, including Steve, laughed at the story.

"Did it work?" he asked with a grin.

She sobered. "Oh, yes. I had no idea what jealousy and possessiveness felt like until then. They aren't comfortable emotions at all!"

Now everyone was gathered in one place, eating her dad's famous barbecue and all the trimmings. She was pleased to see their fathers visiting like old friends and their mothers working side by side to make certain there was plenty of food and drink set out for everyone, young and old.

Her favorite memory of her vacation took place early the morning of the last day of her vacation. She'd been awakened by the sound of Steve's astonished laughter and cursing.

When she opened her eyes she couldn't believe what she saw—her three brothers were standing shoulder to shoulder at the end of the bed, arms folded and looking very dangerous...until she looked at their faces. They were grinning from ear to ear at Steve's reaction to their unexpected presence.

"I told them to fix that alarm so that nobody could bypass it!" he said.

"Can't be done," one of them replied. She didn't remember who it was now.

Steve said, with an attempt at irritation, but he was grinning, too, "If you don't mind, fellows. My fiancée and I are not dressed to be receiving company, just yet. So if you'll excuse us..."

Jason nodded approvingly. "Your fiancée, is it? Well, that's more like it. When are you getting married?"

"She only proposed a few nights ago. We haven't worked out the details as yet."

"*She* proposed! You really are a stubborn ass, aren't you?" Jim said, shaking his head.

"Nope. I learned it from you guys. Now get the hell out of here so we can get dressed."

As it turned out, Robin flew back to Texas with her brothers that afternoon. They had learned that she and Steve had gotten back together from her dad. She had called him when she checked out of the hotel, in case they needed to reach her for any reason, and told him she would be staying with Steve.

Steve and her brothers still chuckled over the stunt,

and she supposed it was funny, but it did give her a start to find them in her bedroom.

"No one knows where we're going for our honeymoon, I hope," she asked Steve now. "That is one place I don't want my brothers showing up."

"As few people as possible. However, Carmela is already making plans to prepare our favorite meals for the next couple of weeks. Ed may have mentioned it to my dad, but I swore them to secrecy where your family was concerned. We don't want those macho maverick brothers of yours showing up again!"

"Thank you for that."

Cindi came up to her and hugged her. "You are a radiant bride, Robin. Thank you for including me in the wedding party."

"Are you kidding? Who else would I have for my maid of honor? You're my sister in every way but blood."

Cindi grinned. "I'm so pleased you two found each other again. Who would have believed when I got engaged that you would be getting married before I do?"

Roger had come with Cindi for the festivities. Robin was amused at how much Roger looked like Jason. He seemed to be a very stable person and crazy about Cindi. It was too bad that Cindi would be living in Chicago while she and Steve were going to be in Los Angeles. She'd probably rack up a bunch of frequent flyer miles between the three areas of California, Illinois and Texas.

"Robin?" her mother called. "It's time for you two to cut the cake."

She looked at Steve. "Are you ready for this?"

"Are you kidding? I've been waiting for you forever. Let's get this over with. There's a tropical island waiting for us."

She kissed him and said, "It won't be long now. We've waited this long. Another few hours will fly by in no time."

She hadn't packed much more for this visit to the island than she'd had with her last time. Clothes weren't really a necessity in that climate.

She intended to keep Steve in his unadorned state as much as possible.

"I'd like to propose a toast," her dad said a few minutes later, "to Mr. and Mrs. Steve Antonelli. May their life together be filled with as much joy, happiness and contentment as I have known with Robin's mom."

Tony stood. "I second that toast. Steve and Robin, may you revel in the blessing of finding your true love, and may you experience the wonder of sharing your life with that person, as I have with Steve's mom." He picked up Susan's hand and kissed it.

"With the examples set before us," Steve replied, "how can we miss?"

*   *   *   *   *

January 2001
TALL, DARK & WESTERN
#1339 by Anne Marie Winston

February 2001
THE WAY TO A RANCHER'S HEART
#1345 by Peggy Moreland

March 2001
MILLIONAIRE HUSBAND
#1352 by Leanne Banks
Million-Dollar Men

April 2001
GABRIEL'S GIFT
#1357 by Cait London
Freedom Valley

May 2001
THE TEMPTATION OF
RORY MONAHAN
#1363 by Elizabeth Bevarly

June 2001
A LADY FOR LINCOLN CADE
#1369 by BJ James
Men of Belle Terre

MAN OF THE MONTH

For twenty years Silhouette has been giving
you the ultimate in romantic reads. Come join
the celebration as some of your favorite authors
help celebrate our anniversary with the most
sensual, emotional love stories ever!

Available at your favorite retail outlet.

Silhouette®
Where love comes alive™

You're not going to believe this offer!

In October and November 2000, buy any two Harlequin or Silhouette books and save $10.00 off future purchases, or buy any three and save $20.00 off future purchases!

Just fill out this form and attach 2 proofs of purchase (cash register receipts) from October and November 2000 books and Harlequin will send you a coupon booklet worth a total savings of $10.00 off future purchases of Harlequin and Silhouette books in 2001. Send us 3 proofs of purchase and we will send you a coupon booklet worth a total savings of $20.00 off future purchases.

Saving money has never been this easy.

I accept your offer! Please send me a coupon booklet:

Name: _____

Address: _____ City: _____

State/Prov.: _____ Zip/Postal Code: _____

Optional Survey!

In a typical month, how many Harlequin or Silhouette books would you buy <u>new</u> at retail stores?

☐ Less than 1   ☐ 1   ☐ 2   ☐ 3 to 4   ☐ 5+

Which of the following statements best describes how you <u>buy</u> Harlequin or Silhouette books? Choose one answer only that <u>best</u> describes you.

☐ I am a regular buyer and reader
☐ I am a regular reader but buy only occasionally
☐ I only buy and read for specific times of the year, e.g. vacations
☐ I subscribe through Reader Service but also buy at retail stores
☐ I mainly borrow and buy only occasionally
☐ I am an occasional buyer and reader

Which of the following statements best describes how you <u>choose</u> the Harlequin and Silhouette series books you buy <u>new</u> at retail stores? By "series," we mean books within a particular line, such as *Harlequin PRESENTS* or *Silhouette SPECIAL EDITION*. Choose one answer only that <u>best</u> describes you.

☐ I only buy books from my favorite series
☐ I generally buy books from my favorite series but also buy books from other series on occasion
☐ I buy some books from my favorite series but also buy from many other series regularly
☐ I buy all types of books depending on my mood and what I find interesting and have no favorite series

Please send this form, along with your cash register receipts as proofs of purchase, to:
In the U.S.: Harlequin Books, P.O. Box 9057, Buffalo, NY 14269
In Canada: Harlequin Books, P.O. Box 622, Fort Erie, Ontario L2A 5X3
(Allow 4-6 weeks for delivery) Offer expires December 31, 2000.   PHQ4002

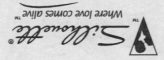